W9-CBW-898

ONCE
UPON
AN
EID

ONCE

UPON

AN

EID

EDITED BY

S. K. Ali AND
Aisha Saee

Stories

of Hope

and Joy

by

15 Muslim

Voices

ILLUSTRATED BY

Sara
Alfageeh

AMULET BOOKS
NEW YORK

Cataloging-in-Publication Data has been applied for and may be obtained from the Library of Congress.

ISBN 978-1-4197-4083-1

Text copyright © 2020 the individual authors
Illustrations copyright © 2020 Sara Alfageeh
Book design by Hana Anouk Nakamura

Printed and bound in U.S.A.
10 9 8 7 6 5 4 3 2 1

Amulet Books are available at special discounts when purchased in quantity for premiums and promotions as well as fundraising or educational use. Special editions can also be created to specification. For details, contact specialsales@abramsbooks.com or the address below.

Amulet Books® is a registered trademark of Harry N. Abrams, Inc.

ABRAMS The Art of Books
195 Broadway, New York, NY 10007
abramsbooks.com

*Bismillah. For all readers who know Eid joy,
and for all who want to share in it.*

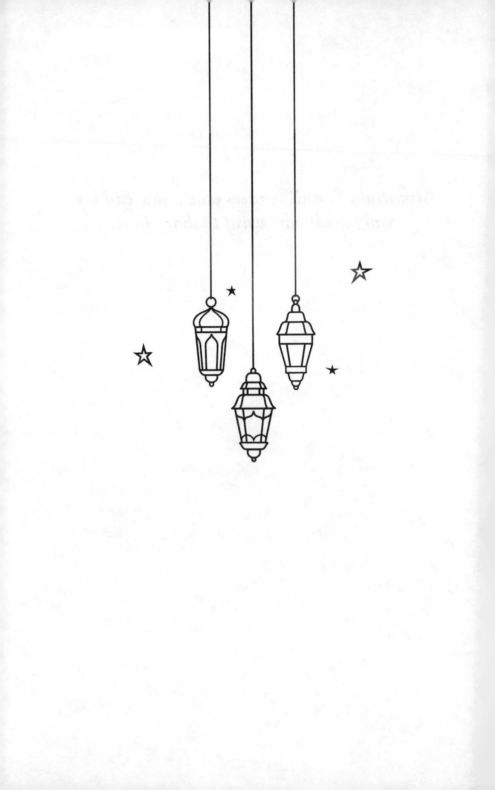

CONTENTS

EDITORS' INTRODUCTION

Dear Readers,

Eid! The short, single-syllable word brings up so many feelings and memories for Muslims. Maybe it's waking up to the sound of frying samosas or the comfort of bean pie; maybe it's the pleasure of putting on a new outfit for Eid prayers or the gift giving, holiday parties, or carnival rides to come that day. Whatever it may be, for most of us who cherish this day of celebration, the emotional responses can be summed up in another short and sweet word: *joy*.

Eid is an Arabic word meaning "celebration/feast that repeats" (i.e., that comes around each year). There are two Eids that are primarily celebrated: Eid-ul-Fitr and Eid-ul-Adha.

Eid-ul-Fitr is the feast of breaking the fast, marking the ending of Ramadan, the month during which many Muslims fast from dawn to sunset. Eid-ul-Adha is the feast of the sacrifice, marking the tenth day of the month of Hajj, during which capable Muslims undertake the pilgrimage to Mecca.

While most countries have adopted the solar calendar, which marks months and years based on the sun,

Muslim holidays follow the lunar calendar, which follows the monthly cycles of the moon. The lunar calendar operates differently from a solar calendar, and as such, Muslim holidays shift by about ten days every year. Thus, readers will see that our Eid stories in this collection take place at different times during the year.

While many people outside of the faith know about Ramadan and Hajj, much of the world does not get to see the joy we feel on Eid in particular. The customs, diverse cultural markers, and family traditions are "insider experiences" seen only within our own communities.

This anthology you are holding opens up this experience to a wide variety of readers—those who celebrate, allowing you to snuggle into the familiar and cozy, and those who don't, allowing you to join in on the celebrating. We hope all feel welcome to the feast of stories we have laid out for you.

There are almost two billion Muslims around the world, and we come from many different walks of life and cultures. As a result, the way that Eid is celebrated can vary from family to family, community to community, culture to culture, and country to country. However, what unites all Muslims during these holidays, from the Uyghur community in Central Asia to the Hui Muslims of China to the large Muslim community in Argentina, is our shared faith and shared joy at celebrating this festive day.

We believe the stories in this anthology capture this mutual joy, and it's for this reason that we are thrilled to share this book with you. Within these pages, you'll meet Hawa, who is nervous about reuniting with her extended family for the Eid holiday in the Bronx. You'll meet Bassem, who is figuring out his first Eid in a refugee community off the coast of Greece, and you'll also meet Adam and Hannah, two siblings sharing a hilarious car ride on the way to celebrate Eid with relatives in Australia.

These are just some of the amazing characters you'll meet in this vibrant collection of stories. We hope the joy will resonate with all kids—Muslims or not—and unite us all in celebration!

With love,

S. K. Ali and Aisha Saeed

Perfect

by Jamilah Thompkins-Bigelow

Mom, Dad, and I got off the bus somewhere in New York City, and it looked like all the people in Philadelphia times ten had been dumped on each block. They must have all been running late, because everyone was speed walking.

I wasn't in any hurry. We were spending Eid here—in a strange city—with new family who didn't act much like family.

Mom tripped after long-legged Dad, a former New Yorker, who strode through the crowds, wheeling a large suitcase. Wearing my lime-green sneakers and a matching hijab that whipped behind me in the spring breeze, I followed with a supermodel strut. I imagined the people rushing past me stopping and cheering for me, Hawa, the twelve-year-old Black American hijabi-nista on the runway!

"Hurry up, Hawa!" Mom yelled. "Stop tryna be cute!"

I ignored her, adding a sashay to my step.

We followed Dad down the steps to a grimy, dark underground station and sprinted toward the roar of an arriving train.

"Train to the Bronx," Dad explained as we hopped inside.

I sat between Dad and Mom, who pulled out her phone and opened up her language app for the tenth time this trip. I couldn't stop myself from rolling my eyes.

"Say it with me: tuh-*nahn*-tay, tuh-*nahn*-tay!" Mom was almost shouting, like Señora Moreno in sixth-grade Spanish.

I repeated her quietly. Maybe I could disappear into my jeans if I stared at them long enough.

"You not even trying, Hawa!"

I looked pleadingly at Dad.

"She's doing okay. Don't worry, Amina," my father said to her, his African accent thick. He patted my braided hair and smiled. "This is my true Mandinka girl."

I didn't feel like a true Mandinka anything, but I smiled back. My father's wide, childlike grin makes me smile even when I don't feel like it.

"Amadou, how she gon' talk to anyone?" Mom asked, her North Philly accent thick too. "Your aunt don't speak a word of English."

Why couldn't Mom stop worrying about Dad's family? Last year, when we first met Dad's side of the family, they weren't worried about Mom. Mom was gripping her phone a bit too tightly. I rubbed the back of her dark headscarf the way she sometimes does to mine. Her grip stayed tight.

"I can talk for us," Dad said. "And Mariama speaks some English. Hawa can talk to Fanta. Fanta speaks perfect—like an American."

I held back a groan.

"I just want Hawa to be proud of all the parts of who she is." Mom looked hard at me. "You are Black American and Mandinka. Both are strong cultures. Love all of you, Hawa."

Mom turned back to her phone, squaring her shoulders and saying the words on her app to herself now.

It was hard to love the idea of spending my Eid with Dad's family from Guinea tomorrow instead of spending it with my best friends, Sanaa and Khalilah. I would miss the park where almost all of Philly's Black American Muslims gathered each Eid to celebrate in their best clothes. I smiled when I thought about my Eid dress: a shimmery coral abaya with a matching jacket so long it reached the floor. I still couldn't believe Mom had let me get it along with a turquoise purse and turquoise sandals! Mom always says I do too much when it comes to color—she likes dark and simple hijabs and abayas.

We were on that rocking train for so long I was almost dozing when Dad shot up from his seat. "We're here!"

I took a deep breath. This year would not be a repeat of the last.

Dad's family was waiting outside the train station: old Mama Dusu (Dad's aunt) and her son, my uncle Kaba; Aunt Mariama (Kaba's wife) and their four little sons; and of course, perfect Fanta. As the adults chattered in

Mandinka and the boys ran in circles, I tried not to look at Fanta, although I felt her looking at me.

Mom grinned at Mama Dusu and Aunt Mariama.

"Assalamu Alaikum. Tuh-*nahn*-tay *la*?" she said slowly and carefully.

Her way of saying it sounded more Philly than African, but Mom was smiling like she had said a magic spell when she asked them how they were doing.

Mama Dusu and Aunt Mariama gasped and then laughed. I squeezed the handle of my suitcase.

"Welcome, my sistuh!" Aunt Mariama said, hugging Mom tightly. Mama Dusu, unspeaking but smiling, took Mom's smooth brown hand with her two wrinkled ones and stared into her eyes, telling her welcome in her own way. I realized then that their laughs were warm, kind ones.

Fanta was laughing too.

I made my eyes into slits, letting her know I wasn't playing any games after what she did last year. Fanta raised her eyebrows, then looked down.

The women began talking fast, with Aunt Mariama slipping back and forth between English and Mandinka to include both women in the conversation. Mom's smile was huge now.

"Come talk to your cousin! Don't be shy!" Dad grabbed my hand and pulled me toward Fanta.

"Uncle Amadou, I missed you!" Fanta squealed. Then, as if I were a little girl and not her same age, she exclaimed, "And Hawa, you're almost as tall as me now!"

I gritted out a grin. "Almost!"

I was nowhere close. I had inherited my mother's short roundedness—not like Dad's family, who all had long, thin bodies.

"You two look more alike each day. Both so beautiful!" Dad continued. Fanta looked down. She probably knew he really meant her. Fanta had the kind of face that YouTubers show you how to paint on, with all the contours, except she didn't have any makeup on. Her dark skin glowed naturally. My dark skin was just dark—no glow. Mom calls my features "striking." I have too-big eyes, a too-big nose, and much-too-large lips crammed into a small face. I do have an amazing walk though.

We trudged a few blocks to their building and went up in a dim elevator that smelled like spices that had sat there too long.

A fresher smell of tender meat, stewed tomatoes, fried onions, fragrant peppers, and sweet cabbage filled their apartment. It was the last day of Ramadan; however, traveling Muslims don't have to fast, so Aunt Mariama had cooked jollof rice for us. Smiling, she handed us large bowls. I dug in, stuffing a heaping spoonful into my mouth. The tender beef melted on my tongue.

I scooped up another spoonful with a strange-looking string bean. I gagged, coughing up my food into a paper towel. My whole mouth was burning. Mom was taking small bites and discreetly drinking sips of water after each one. Dad, though, was quickly clearing his bowl.

"They aren't used to it," Dad explained. "I use mild spices at home and for Americans at my restaurant—I add the strong ones for the Africans." I almost asked Dad, wasn't I supposed to be African too? So much for being a perfect Mandinka girl.

Aunt Mariama looked pained.

"It's good, Aunt Mariama," I said. I nibbled on a small spoonful, blinking back the tears in my eyes.

"If you can't take spice, have plantains. I made them," Fanta suggested with that smile again.

"Thanks," I mumbled. The sweet, soft plantains did help, and that annoyed me. How could a girl my age make plantains like that?

"Fanta, you cooking already?" Mom asked.

"Yes!" Fanta's eyes lit up. "I love cooking. I'm baking cupcakes for Eid!"

"She used to watch me cook and learned how to cook African food. Now she watches cooking shows and cooks American foods too," Aunt Mariama explained, pride in her voice.

"Could you teach me how to cook soul food, Aunt Amina?" Fanta asked.

"Of course!" Mom exclaimed.

I had to hand it to my cousin: No one was a better suck-up.

"You hear that, Hawa?" Mom said. "It's time you learned how to cook too."

"No, thanks," I said.

Fanta looked away, then stared at the floor.

Mom glared at me until I looked away. I knew I was being rude, but I couldn't stop myself.

After our meal, Mama Dusu, Aunt Mariama, and Fanta took Mom and me into a bedroom.

Fanta explained, "Mama Dusu made our Eid clothes!"

"But I already have—"

Mom stopped me with a stern look.

Spread out on a large bed were two outfits with golden bangles and earrings beside them. One was a large gown and skirt made of shiny brown fabric with a basic golden pattern in a simple, elegant style like Mom's. And the other was a fitted top and matching skirt, which popped with a rainbow of colors moving in wild spirals.

Mama Dusu smiled proudly.

"How did she know our sizes?" Mom asked skeptically.

"Amadou told us! We wanted to surprise you," Aunt Mariama replied. "Fanta and I picked out the fabric!"

I waited for Mom to say thanks but no thanks—that as nice as these were, we already had outfits. Mom started blubbering instead.

"Thank you," she whispered through her tears. Then Aunt Mariama started crying and Mama Dusu too. Then they were all hugging and talking fast again. I wanted to yell, "Wait a minute! I already have the perfect dress!"

"Try it on!" Aunt Mariama said, lifting at the hem of Mom's tunic. Mom allowed Aunt Mariama to undress her down to her slip and underwear like it was the most natural thing ever.

Fanta smiled that smile again. "You want to try yours on too?"

No way would I let Miss Perfect see my rolls. I snatched up the outfit and asked, "Where's the bathroom?"

"We're all women . . ." Aunt Mariama began, and then stopped. "Down at the end of the hall." Aunt Mariama looked at Fanta, giving an order with her eyes.

"Do you need help?" Fanta asked.

"No, thank you," I said.

She looked down, frowning.

In the bathroom, I put the blouse on first, a top that flared out like a mini dress. I wrapped the scarf around my head like Aunt Mariama's as best I could. I put on the earrings and bangles and looked in the mirror. I looked . . . good—so surprisingly good I had to smile.

I tried wrapping the lapa, a long, wide cloth with no fasteners or strings. I tried two times, but each time the skirt fell down as soon as I moved. The third time, I wrapped it as tightly as I could—so tight it squeezed my waist.

"Are you okay in there?" Aunt Mariama called. I heard her fuss to Fanta, "I told you to help your cousin."

"I'm fine!" I said, opening the door. Mama Dusu, Aunt Mariama, Fanta, and Mom were standing right outside. Mom looked stunning in her flowing gown.

Mom gasped. "Gorgeous!"

Maybe I would think about wearing this outfit for Eid. Maybe.

I took a step forward and toppled face-first to the floor. I couldn't move my legs at all.

"Are you okay? We have to show you how to wrap it . . ." Aunt Mariama said, trying to help me up, humor in her eyes. The four of them looked at each other and then exploded into laughter.

"Hawa, I'm sorry," Mom said, trying to catch her breath.

I wriggled to my feet and took pigeon-toed steps back into the bathroom, which made them laugh harder. Shutting the door, I yanked off the lapa, blouse, head covering, and jewelry. I wasn't wearing any of it for Eid.

That night, after Fanta's rowdy brothers were put to bed, the adults went to the last Ramadan prayer service at the mosque up the street. Fanta was puttering around the kitchen, and I went into her bedroom. We would be sharing it that night. I noticed another outfit of shiny purple fabric hanging up on the closet door—Fanta's dress. I decided to pull out my own Eid clothes to make sure there weren't any wrinkles. I took the coral abaya out of my suitcase and laid it out on the bed. I was just about to take out the matching jacket when Fanta walked in with two plates, a chocolate cupcake on each.

"I snuck us some early Eid treats," she said, pressing a plate into my hand. She noticed my abaya, and her face dropped.

She plastered on her usual smile and said, "I was just going to show you how to wear your lapa."

"I already have an outfit," I said.

She gaped, then glared. "Why are you always like this?"

"Like what? I just want to wear my own dress."

"You think you're too good for us."

"*Me?* I'm not the one always acting like Miss Perfect!"

"What does that even mean? I try to be nice, but you're never nice back!"

"Nice? You? You upset my mom last time we were here!"

"How? She didn't say anything the whole time she was here. Neither did you!"

I imitated her mousy voice. "You don't speak Mandinka? No French? Only English? Ha-ha-ha."

"I didn't mean it like—"

I continued to mock her. "You're the only child? Africans don't do that! Ha-ha-ha."

"I didn't say that to your mom!"

"You said it to *me,* and you all laughed, and she heard you! At least we don't have a bajillion kids in one little apartment!"

"Wait a minute!" Fanta snapped.

"At least we're not too good to eat your greasy food! You and your mom didn't even touch Mom's food last time, and she was up all night making it! We ate your nasty, oily plantains anyway!"

"Stop! Stop! Stop! That's not nice!" Fanta yelled, flailing her arms. A cupcake flew onto the bed, right smack-dab in the middle of my abaya.

She gasped. "Oh! I didn't mean to!"

With a growl, I lunged at her. She turned to run,

but I tackled her fast. I mashed cake into her face again and again.

"Get off!" Fanta threw me off of her.

She swiped the cake from her face and held me down as she smeared it on mine. I twisted around to get free, dropping my plate.

I leapt to the bed. Standing on top of it, I grabbed two gobs of cake from my abaya and wound up my arm like a pitcher.

"No!" Fanta shrieked.

I lobbed both chunks at the outfit hanging on the closet. She snatched my plate from the floor. I dodged one chocolaty throw, then another, but one hit me square in the nose. Fanta pointed and cackled.

I wiped my nose. "Well, you look a mess too!"

She touched her face, smearing even more icing on it. I laughed then.

I scooped cake off of my face. Licking it, I said, "You cook as good as you throw."

We both laughed then, laughed until we fell onto the bed, laughed until we were crying.

"I'm sorry," she finally said.

"Me too."

"No, not just for this. For last year. We didn't know much English when we met you. I said some mean things so I wouldn't feel stupid."

"We were embarrassed too, so we didn't talk. I'm half Mandinka. I should know some words."

"You're lucky to have two cultures."

"My mom says I need to love both of them."

"Your mom is smart—nice too. I said that thing about Africans having lots of kids because I was jealous. You get your mom and a whole house to yourself, and we're all crammed into this apartment."

"Mom can't have kids easy. I'm her miracle," I said quietly.

"We learned that later. Uncle Amadou was so upset. We've been trying to make it up to Aunt Amina . . . and you."

"Well, what do we do now?" I asked. Chocolate was on the walls and floor. My abaya and her gown were ruined.

"Our parents are going to kill us!"

"Not if they don't know anything. Where do you keep your cleaning supplies?"

We scrubbed the floor and walls, and the room looked normal in minutes. I washed the stains out of Fanta's purple gown and my abaya in the bathroom sink.

Fanta wrung them out and sighed. "They won't be dry in time for tomorrow."

I had an idea and ran into Fanta's room. I took down the lapa that had been behind her gown and placed it next to my untouched shimmery jacket. Cute!

✳ ✳ ✳

The next morning, Fanta spun around in her purple lapa and my coral jacket, which came down past her knees. "I'm beautiful like you now!"

"Me? You're the pretty, perfect one!"

"Oh, please! Everyone knows you're the pretty one, Hawa," Fanta said, and she meant it.

"Squat down low," she said while wrapping my lapa as tight as possible. When I stood, the skirt was wound tightly around my waist, but I walked easily. I looked amazing in Fanta's full-length mirror, and yet something was missing. I found the turquoise shoes and matching purse in my suitcase. Their color popped with my African outfit.

We celebrated Eid in a park in the Bronx where many other West Africans went, wearing dazzling colors against dark skin. Food was spread out on tables—many African dishes and sweets and also Hawa's cupcakes and the bean pies Mom had made from an old family recipe. Mom was radiant as she laughed with Aunt Mariama and Mama Dusu, who was eating her third slice of bean pie. And I knew then what Mom meant about loving all of me.

Fanta introduced me to two of her friends, whose looks reminded me of Sanaa and Khalilah.

Without thinking, I said, "Tuh-*nahn*-tay *la*?"

"Tanasté!" they replied.

Fanta smiled. At first I thought she was mocking me, but then I realized her smile was warm and kind—maybe it always had been.

Fanta spoke: "The way you said that . . . it was . . . perfect."

Yusuf and the Great Big Brownie Mistake

by Aisha Saeed

Eid lights twinkled along the curved entrance of our family room. Our last Ramadan meal now behind us, everyone was hurrying to finish up last-minute preparations for Eid. My father arranged the wrapped presents by the fireplace. My nani sat on the rocker next to him, hemming the kamiz my big sister, Roshan, was wearing the next morning.

And me? I was helping my mother make our traditional Eid brownies for brunch the next day. Roshan stood across from me on the other side of the island, layering blueberries on the tart she'd spent all evening working on. This was the first year she wasn't making Eid brownies with us.

It was her loss, I reminded myself. The tart would probably taste fine—as good as a dessert with *fruit* in it could—but it wasn't exactly a secret that Eid brownies were our family's favorite dessert.

"Ready?" my mother asked me. A red apron was tied around her waist, and she held a white mixing spoon in her hand.

Roshan glanced over at us. "Eid brownie time?"

"Feeling jealous?" I teased her.

"Yeah, I'm jealous when *I'm* the one who decided to move on," she retorted.

"Come on now, the more dessert the better, in my opinion," my mother said. She pulled her cooking binder off the shelf and flipped to the brownie recipe.

"We don't need that," I told her. "I know the recipe by heart."

"Can't be too careful with one of the most important items on the menu."

Well, that was true. We got to work quickly, sifting the flour and cocoa, cracking eggs, and melting the butter before stirring it all together. My mom liked to pull out photos from when I was a little kid with powder all over my face from the mixing, but now I was eleven and there wasn't so much as a speck of dust on me.

"How's it going?" my father asked, stepping into the kitchen. He looked over my sister's shoulder. "Roshan, that dessert looks too pretty to eat."

"The blueberries won't stay still." Roshan frowned. "They wiggle every time I try to pick up the tart."

"The cream will set in the fridge, and you can re-adjust the berries in the morning," my mother called out to her.

"But we all know the *brownies* will taste the best," I said with a grin.

"Do you hear him?" Roshan complained.

"Yusuf." My father reached over and mussed my hair.

"What?" I asked. "No one's ever made a tart before. Eid brownies are called Eid brownies for a reason."

"Roshan worked hard," my mother said. "I'm sure it's going to taste delicious."

I didn't reply. It made no sense. How could she just decide she was suddenly too old to be part of a family tradition from as far back as I could remember?

"I think the batter is ready to be poured into the pan." My mother put a hand on my shoulder and looked down at the metal mixing bowl. "Are you sure you don't want to bake them now? Tomorrow's a busy day."

"Brownies fresh out of the oven taste the best," I said. When I was little, she had baked the brownies the night before, but for the past two years I had tweaked the tradition and baked them the day of Eid. The smell of cocoa drifting through the house had a way of making the whole day feel a little more special.

"Fine. But that means the brownies are your responsibility tomorrow, got it?" she said. "We're hosting close to fifty people this year, so getting them baked, cut, and set on the dessert table will be your job."

"I can do it," I promised.

I poured the brownie batter into the pan and covered it with plastic wrap before tucking it in the fridge behind the marinating chicken for biryani tomorrow and the sweet round gulab jamans my grandmother had spent the morning frying.

In just a few hours it would be Eid.

I couldn't wait.

✳ ✳ ✳

The prayer hall was packed by the time we got to the masjid the next morning. People mingled and chatted and talked over one another while two men walked through the aisles with orange Fitrana donation boxes. Even with the crowds I still managed to find my best friend, Eesa, and his father sitting on their prayer rugs toward the front of the room. As soon as he saw me in the distance, he waved us over. My father and I spread our rugs next to theirs and settled down.

"Coming to our place after this?" I asked him.

"Yep! Right after we open our gifts, and"—he leaned in—"I'm pretty sure my parents got me the Nintendo Switch for Eid!"

"No way! How do you know?"

"It's the only thing I asked for. And I said it could double as my Eid *and* birthday gift since it's so expensive. I did all my homework on time, I got one hundreds on my last two math tests, and I've cleaned out Tesla's litter box all month without even being asked. And this morning there was a wrapped package sitting on the dining table with all the other gifts that's the *exact* same size as a Nintendo Switch box. So . . ." He shrugged and grinned.

"And it's portable," I told him. "Maybe you can bring it to our house?"

"Definitely!" he replied as Imam Yaseen rose to begin Eid prayers. We lined up shoulder to shoulder. The thought of possibly playing *Super Mario Odyssey* and eating fresh-baked brownies in just a little while meant this was shaping up to be one of the best Eids ever.

When we arrived home, the smells of cardamom, cinnamon, and cloves tickled my nose. My grandmother had stayed back to finish making the biryani, and now the freshly layered onions and rice and chicken resting on the wide serving pan made my mouth water.

The doorbell rang. My father's sister, Phupo Saira, had arrived. My twin cousins squealed as they ran straight for the family room and my box of old toys.

Roshan pulled her dessert out of the fridge, and I winced. My mom had said the cream would set in the fridge, but the tart looked like a Salvador Dalí creation of droopy blueberries, kiwi, and strawberries. The thing about brownies—I pulled my pan out of the fridge—was they didn't need to look pretty. They tasted great just the way they were.

I set the oven to 350 degrees and stuck the brownies in as the doorbell rang and more and more people arrived, the house filling with the sounds of conversation and laughter. I glanced at the clock: 11:00 a.m. on the dot. At 11:25, I'd pull out the perfect Eid brownies.

In the dining room, I grabbed the serving platter, and the doorbell chimed again. It was Eesa and his parents!

And in his hands was the Nintendo Switch box. I set down the tray and hurried upstairs to the loft. We flipped on the television. It took a while to figure out how to get the Switch to cast to the TV and to get our Miis to look like us, but it was worth it, because when we began the game, it actually felt like we were *inside the game.*

"This is incredible," I said under my breath as we dove further and further into Mario's Odyssey. "My dad doesn't think we need the Switch. He's too attached to his Super Nintendo where Mario is just eating mush-rooms all day long . . ."

I lowered the control.

I looked at the wall clock over the television.

I read the time: 11:35 a.m.

That couldn't be right.

"I'll be back," I said before jumping up and racing down the stairs.

I flung open the oven door and grabbed the mitts.

I yanked out the brownies.

But it was too late.

They were burned.

The edges were charred black.

Instead of being springy and soft, the top layer of chocolate cracked under my fingers like a potato chip.

This was the one dish I was in charge of. The most important one. And I'd ruined it.

Just then, my grandmother came in from the dining

room and put a hand on my shoulder. "What's with that face?" she asked me.

"I messed up the brownies." A tear slipped down my cheek. "They're destroyed."

"Well, they're definitely a bit black on the edges." She studied the pan. "But destroyed? Hardly. I know the perfect way to fix them."

She went to the pantry and brought back a container of chocolate frosting. "Yours isn't the first dessert to hit a snag," she told me. "But frosting makes most desserts taste better. Spread some along the edges, and no one will know a thing."

I pulled a knife out of the cutlery drawer and edged the brownies with frosting. They didn't look quite so burned now, but they still didn't look edible.

"Yusuf!" a voice gasped. "What did you do?" It was Roshan. She stared at me. My chest tightened. I had teased her yesterday about her dessert, and now I'd ruined my own. She looked down at the tray and shook her head. And then, before I could reply, she walked away. Probably to tell our mother. I'd be on pots and pans cleanup duty until I was eighteen now.

Just then my father walked into the kitchen holding a half-empty tray of biryani.

"What's going on?" he asked me.

"No brownies this year," I said softly. My father loved Eid brownies. He normally dove into them before he'd even had his meal, like I did. "I lost track of time. Nani said the frosting could cover up the black edges, but they still look awful."

"Hmmm." My father scratched his beard. "Frosting is good, but whipped cream helps too." He walked to the fridge and brought back a container of Cool Whip. "Add some dollops in the middle, and between that and the fudge edges, I think it'll be just fine."

I pulled out a spoon and added puffs of whipped cream like he said. He was right. With the iced edges and the whipped cream center, it looked like I was trying my hand at decorating. You couldn't tell the brownies were burned anymore. But how would they taste?

Just then Roshan walked back over and stood next to me.

"You sure messed that up." She looked down at the brownies. "Take this." She handed me a ziplock bag of M&M'S.

I stared at the bag. "Why?"

"It's my secret stash." She rolled her eyes. "If you make a pattern with them or just sprinkle them on the Cool Whip, it'll add a little extra sweetness to each bite and make it look like you did all this on purpose."

"You would do that for me?"

"Well, it *is* Eid." She poked me with her elbow.

"Thanks," I told her. "The tart looked good."

"That's sweet of you to say, Yusuf." She sighed. "But

it definitely doesn't look like the Pinterest picture, and no amount of M&M'S will fix it."

"It doesn't have to look like that picture," I told her. "You can get one like that photo at any old bakery. Yours looks like art. It's one of a kind."

"One of a kind, yes. But art?" Roshan shook her head. But she laughed as she carried the tart over to the dessert table just outside the kitchen.

Just then my mother walked in.

"How's it going?" she asked. She glanced at the brownies and tilted her head. "Went for a different look this year?"

I knew she'd notice. How could she not? Brownies were part of *her* childhood Eid tradition. She had baked them with my grandmother each year since she was a kid.

"I burned them." I looked down at the counter. "I lost track of time. Nani gave me icing. Abu got me whipped cream. Roshan shared her M&M'S, but it doesn't matter. They're not the Eid brownies we make, and they definitely won't taste good." I swallowed. "I'm sorry I ruined our tradition."

My mother picked up the butter knife resting on the counter and cut out a small square. She took a bite. She closed her eyes. When she opened them, she looked at me.

"Have you tried them?" she asked.

I shook my head.

"Go ahead." She cut another square and handed it to me.

I took it from her and prepared for the worst, but . . .

"They taste good!" I exclaimed. "They're different." I glanced down at the tray. "I burned them so bad I thought they were destroyed."

"When I was not much older than you are now, I also messed up the Eid brownies. After that, your grandmother always made sure to have plenty of adjustment tools on hand, just in case."

I sliced the brownies, placed them on the serving platter, carried them out to the dining table, and set them next to a tray of chocolate chip cookies and my nani's gulab jaman.

Roshan was standing by the table.

"Trade you a brownie for a slice of tart?" I asked her. I glanced over at her tart plate—but the plate was empty!

"That fast?" I said. "Must've been pretty delicious."

"You can tell me yourself," she said. "I saved you a slice." She pulled a plate out of the china cabinet and handed it to me.

I took a bite. "Wow. It's fantastic," I told her. And I meant it. "Who knew fruit in a dessert could taste so good?"

"Seriously?" She frowned. "Everyone here's going to tell me it's good because they don't want to discourage me, you know? Do you like it? Honestly?"

"I do," I said. "It's creamy and sweet and just a little tangy. Maybe we could have it again for next Eid."

"Make it a new part of the dessert tradition?"

"Yeah." I hesitated. "And maybe next time we could make our desserts—both of them—together?"

"Yeah." She smiled. "Maybe we could."

I finished the tart and grabbed two brownies before hurrying back up to the loft, where Eesa was waiting for me.

"Hey," he said when I sat down next to him. "Everything okay?"

I handed him a brownie and picked up my controller.

"Everything is great." I smiled.

And it was.

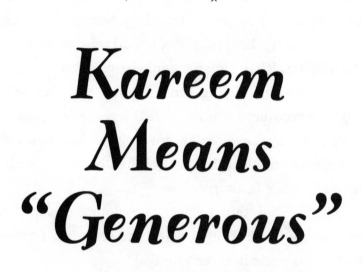

Kareem Means "Generous"

by Asmaa Hussein

Kareem wiped his sweaty forehead with his sleeve. Mr. Johnson's unruly lawn was tamed at last.

At the end of winter, Kareem had outgrown his old bike. He was already as tall as his dad! To save up for a Super Speedster X (and a matching helmet, if he made enough money), he'd been doing odd jobs all Ramadan: watering Mr. Khan's plants while he traveled to visit his son in Pakistan, buying groceries for Ms. Donaldson while she recovered from a broken leg, and washing Mr. Adler's muddy car after he drove up to the mountains for a hiking trip. But this last job had been the hardest, especially while fasting.

"Here's your ten dollars," Mr. Johnson said. "My wife's going to be thrilled when she sees this. I haven't mowed this beast in three months!"

"Thanks, Mr. Johnson!" Kareem said, sliding the bill into his pocket. "Call me if you have any other chores that need doing!"

Just as Kareem arrived home, his dad called from the kitchen, "Iftaar time!"

Kareem was starving. He nearly dove headfirst into the lentil soup, koshari, and roasted chicken his mom had cooked for their evening meal. Breaking his fast had never felt so good!

"Uhh, can you please take two seconds to say bismillah before stuffing your face?" Mom said.

"Oops," Kareem said with stuffed chipmunk cheeks. "Bismillah."

Kareem noticed Dad tapping his pencil against a notepad full of illegible scribbles.

"What's wrong, Dad?" Kareem asked. "You seem distracted."

Dad sighed. "I have designer's block . . . It's like writer's block, except for graphic designers. I just can't figure out what angle to take for this company's advertising campaign. My pitch is on Monday."

"What do you have so far?" Kareem asked.

Dad cleared his throat. "OutStride Biking Equipment Limited: Everything you need for a great ride."

"Dad, that's so basic," said Kareem.

"I know," groaned Dad. "Okay, brainstorm with me. What's the first word that comes to mind when I say *biking*?"

"Athletes! Races! Olympics!" Kareem said.

"The Olympics . . . That could actually work!" Dad furiously scribbled something onto his notepad.

"So, Kareem, I ran into Kim from across the hall today," Mom said, casually changing the subject. "Her son, Shawn, is starting a paper route tomorrow morning."

Oh no. Kareem could see the wheels turning in Mom's head. She'd been trying to get him to hang out with Shawn for two weeks just because he was the new kid in class. Shawn seemed nice enough in school, but Kareem already had friends.

"I volunteered your services." Mom tucked her hair behind her ears. "Shawn still doesn't know the neighborhood that well. You can show him all the shortcuts on his first day."

Kareem groaned. "But why? It's not *my* paper route! I've been doing so many chores for bike money. All I want to do is sleep in tomorrow."

"I know," said Mom, "but it's the considerate thing to do, and it's just for one morning."

Kareem could tell from the determined look on Mom's face that she wouldn't let this go.

"Fiiine."

Kareem's mom nudged him awake at 5:00 a.m.

"Time for suhoor," she whispered. "And you're meeting Shawn in half an hour."

Kareem rubbed his eyes and sat up in bed. *God, I'd better get a pile of good deed credits for this.*

At the kitchen table, Kareem inhaled fuul, pita bread, and yogurt before the call to Fajr prayer. A big stack of letters sat on the counter.

"Kareem, something came for you in the mail yesterday. I think it's from Teta," said Mom.

Kareem's grandma was the best. She only visited once a year, but she was always sending him funny cards, old photos, and newspaper clippings that made her laugh. He ripped the envelope open and pulled out a purple Eid greeting card. Two crisp green twenty-dollar bills slipped out and fluttered to the ground.

"Forty dollars?!" shouted Kareem, setting the card down. "Do you know what this means? No more chores! I can finally buy my bike!" He jumped around the room as though he were bouncing on a giant trampoline.

Mom opened the card and read Teta's message out loud:

Dear Kareem,

   Early Eid Mubarak, habibi! Did you know your name means "generous"? Think about doing something generous with this money for Eid, will ya?

   Love, Teta

Kareem stopped. "Wait, what does that mean?"

"Well, lots of people won't have an elaborate Eid celebration like we will," Mom said. "Maybe that money can bring some happiness to another family."

Kareem crossed his arms and stood quietly for a moment. *I've been working so hard for a new bike. I deserve this money more than* anyone.

"Anyway." Mom shrugged. "Teta sent the money to *you*, so you decide for yourself."

"I've decided to generously buy *myself* the best Eid gift ever!" Kareem did a perfect cartwheel, crammed the bills into his pocket, and twirled out the door.

"So, your mom forced you to come on my paper route with me, eh?" Shawn smirked as he unlocked his bike outside their building. His oversized Montreal Canadiens baseball hat covered most of his forehead.

"Yeah, kinda. I was already awake for suhoor, though," Kareem said. "That's the meal we eat before we start fasting."

"Cool. Well, thanks for coming anyway," said Shawn.

"No problem," Kareem grunted.

"So, are you a Leafs fan?" Shawn asked. "Because if you are, we can't be friends."

"Nah," Kareem replied. "Hockey isn't my thing. But I am a Raptors fan."

Shawn chuckled as he stacked what looked like fifty newspapers into his bike basket. "All right, I can deal with that."

"Aren't those heavy?" Kareem asked.

"Yeah, but I'm used to it. I had a paper route in Montreal before I moved here," Shawn said. "The basket makes it easier to manage, even if I just push the bike instead of riding today."

The dawn light inched up the horizon as Shawn and Kareem made their way through the delivery list. Each time they stopped at a house, Shawn walked a few steps into the front yard and carefully tossed a newspaper onto the porch. Then Kareem impatiently crossed the house off the list. The faster they finished, the faster Kareem could grab the money he'd saved and get to the bike shop.

Halfway through the route, the boys came up to a house surrounded by a chain-link fence. Two fat recycling bins sat in the middle of the sidewalk. Shawn pushed his bike onto the quiet road and parked it at the curb in front of the bins.

Newspaper in hand, he walked toward the gate, but he hesitated when he saw a clumsy handwritten note taped to a tiny doghouse on the lawn: "Beware of Dog!"

Just as Shawn's hand touched the edge of the fence, a Chihuahua lunged out of the doghouse and yipped so loudly that both Shawn and Kareem jumped backward. They collided with each other, then, like dominoes, knocked down the recycling bins and Shawn's bike.

"Ahh!" yelled Kareem. "Stupid dog! How could such a loud sound come out of such a tiny body?"

"Hah! I've seen way worse dogs on my other paper routes," Shawn said, standing up and brushing the dust off his pants. "At least this one's behind a fence! Let's pick up all this stuff before the owners notice."

Kareem righted the bins and collected some of the things that had fallen out of them.

Crash! Kareem and Shawn whipped their heads around.

A rusty gray car screeched to a halt right where Shawn's bike had been. The bike slid across the pavement. An angry balding man threw open his car door.

"Hey! Get that piece of junk out of the road!"

"You hit my bike!" Shawn yelled. He ran toward the mess of twisted bike parts and scattered newspapers.

"Blame yourself," the man retorted, examining the front of his car. "It's not my fault you left your bike in the middle of the road. You should be glad it didn't damage my car!"

Without another word, the man jumped into his car and sped off.

Shawn lowered himself onto his knees next to his bike. His head hung down as he examined the bent wheel and twisted handlebar.

"I can't ride it like this!" he said.

"I'm so sorry, Shawn . . . Hey, it doesn't look that bad!" Kareem lied. *Aw, man, it looks totally wrecked.*

"Kareem, do you think you could . . ."

"What?"

"Do you think you could finish my paper route for me while I wheel the bike home? There are only seven houses left."

Kareem froze. *How could he ask me to finish* his *paper route? I shouldn't even be here at all!*

"Uhh, I don't think that's a good idea," Kareem replied, grasping for an excuse. "I'm probably going to make mistakes. Can't we just go straight home?"

"I'll get in trouble if I don't finish the route," Shawn said. He looked around uncertainly. "I guess I can just leave the bike on the sidewalk, and we'll come get it when we're done."

Shawn quickly collected the remaining newspapers, stuffing them into his messenger bag, and then dragged the damaged bike onto the sidewalk.

They walked on in silence. The neighborhood was still asleep, and everything was quiet except for the sound of a distant rumbling garbage truck.

After Shawn delivered the final paper on his route, the boys sprinted back toward the house with the chain-link fence. Like clockwork, the Chihuahua started barking right as they turned the corner and spotted the house.

But something wasn't right. The bike was gone!

They frantically searched behind the recycling bins and between the bushes.

"We left it right here!" Shawn panted. "Where is it? Do you think someone stole it?"

Kareem lifted the lids of the recycling bins and peered inside. *Oh God, no. This can't be happening.*

"The bins are empty." He gulped. "The truck must have come by while we were gone. They probably thought the bike was junk too."

Shawn let out a groan and kicked the curb hard. He pulled his baseball cap over his face and sat down next to the empty bins.

Kareem shoved his hands into his pockets. An uncomfortable sadness tugged at his throat. *This wasn't supposed to happen. I was just going to show him some shortcuts, then split!*

"Hey," Kareem said awkwardly. "Maybe your mom will get you a new bike."

"No. She spent all her savings on stuff for the new apartment," Shawn replied. "My dad won't help either. He still lives in Montreal and doesn't like it when I ask him for money."

Ugh, what was I thinking? That was such a dumb thing to say.

The boys trudged home in silence.

"Let me know what your mom says," Kareem mumbled as they stepped into the elevator.

Shawn replied with a low grunt. " 'Kay."

At home, Kareem threw himself onto his bed and

yawned. His whole body felt strangely itchy, and he couldn't get the image of Shawn out of his head.

It's not my fault his bike got thrown away. It was just an accident.

But every time Kareem tried closing his eyes, all he saw was Shawn sitting on the sidewalk with his baseball cap over his face.

On Monday morning, just five days before Eid, Kareem clipped his helmet straps shut and rode his new bike to school. Mom had taken him shopping over the weekend. She'd chosen a sparkly Eid banner and gold balloons at Party City, and Kareem had gotten his bike at Canadian Tire. The best part was standing at the store register and finding out that the bike was on sale, so he didn't even have to use the forty dollars Teta had sent him! Kareem planned to go back to the store after school to buy a new helmet. His old one was scuffed and didn't match the shiny new bike.

Just as Kareem had anticipated, the ride to school was as smooth as butter. A cool breeze hit his face and hugged the back of his neck. *This is the life.*

"Good morning, class!" Mrs. Waters chirped at the start of first period.

Halfway through attendance, the door creaked open,

and Shawn crept into the room. He quickly slid into the seat right in front of Kareem. Shawn's shoelaces were undone, and the back of his neck was coated with beads of sweat.

He must have been running. Is he late because of his paper route? Kareem wondered.

When the period two bell rang, Mrs. Waters stopped in front of Shawn's desk. "Shawn, I know you're still a bit new here, but I expect my students to be on time."

Shawn nodded. "Sorry, I'll try my best to get here earlier."

Kareem watched Shawn fiddle with his pencil case as they waited for the math teacher. Kareem poked him.

"Hey, Shawn!"

Shawn turned. "Oh, hey, Kareem."

"Did you miss the bus?"

"No. They added five new houses to my paper route. I kinda miscalculated how long it would take to get around without a bike."

"Oh, yeah, that must be hard." *Just say it already. You'll feel better.* "I'm sorry. I should have just finished the paper route for you that day."

"It's not your fault." Shawn shrugged. "I think it was just bad luck. If I leave home half an hour earlier, I can deliver the newspapers and get to school on time."

Kareem was shocked. "Half an hour earlier? But you already leave home before sunrise!"

"It's temporary," Shawn replied. "I'm saving for a new bike. I should be able to get one in a few weeks."

The math teacher walked in before Kareem could say anything more. What would he have said, anyway? Shawn looked exhausted, and there was nothing Kareem could do about it.

At the end of the day, Kareem zipped open his backpack in front of his locker. Something purple slipped out of his bag and landed on the ground.

Teta's Eid Mubarak card. *Is this card haunting me? No, it probably just got stuck in one of my notebooks.*

Kareem opened and reread it: "Did you know your name means 'generous'?" He angrily shoved the card back into his bag. *I know what my name means! But it's too late now. I'm buying my helmet!*

Kareem got onto his bike and rode until he was in front of Canadian Tire. He ran to the back of the store and scanned the helmets hanging on the racks. He picked one up and admired its sleek black and red stripes. It looked perfect, but it felt heavier than normal.

Too heavy.

Helmet in hand, Kareem wandered through the aisles for a while until he reached the sports equipment section and noticed a big red sign that read CLEARANCE.

Kareem rifled through some of the knickknacks on the shelf, and then he noticed a box pushed all the way to the back. The man on the box was riding a bicycle with a large basket hooked onto the front of it. The basket was full of groceries, a bouquet of flowers, and a tiny dog.

A shiver ran up Kareem's spine. He stared at the box for a few seconds. *This delivery basket would be perfect for Shawn . . . if he had a bike.*

He stared longingly at the shiny new helmet in one hand and the delivery basket in the other. He could only afford one.

Knock, knock, knock.

Kareem stood at Shawn's door at 5:15 the next morning. He was about to knock again when he heard shuffling coming from inside. Shawn swung the door open. His hair was messy, and his eyes looked heavy and tired. He was wearing only one shoe.

"Uhh . . . hi," Kareem stammered. "Sorry for knocking so early, but I figured you'd be awake."

"Hi," Shawn replied, stifling a massive yawn. "What's up?" He bent down to put his other shoe on.

"You can borrow my bike for your paper route," Kareem blurted. "I hung a big delivery basket on the front for the newspapers."

Shawn's mouth hung open. "Wow," he said slowly. "I mean, that's really generous of you, but don't you ride your bike to school?"

"Yeah. But I planned the whole thing out already," Kareem said. "You'll take my bike in the morning for your paper route, then ride it straight to school and lock it up outside. After school, I'll pick it up and ride it home. Easy."

Shawn nodded. "Yeah, but how are *you* getting to school in the morning?"

"Bus," Kareem said. He suppressed a shudder at the word. He hated taking the bus, but he couldn't stand the thought of Shawn waking up in the dead of night like this.

On Friday afternoon, Kareem arrived home from school to find Mom hanging up the Eid banner with the phone perched between her shoulder and her ear.

"Eid is tomorrow!" Mom said, throwing her arms around Kareem and squeezing tight. "Oh, and Teta's on the phone for you."

"Assalamu Alaikum, Teta! Eid Mubarak!" Kareem grinned into the receiver.

"Walaikumussalaam, Kareem! How's my favorite grandson?"

"I'm your only grandson!" He laughed. Teta liked using that joke a lot. "Alhamdulillah, Teta. How are you?"

They chatted for a while about what they were each going to do for Eid. Then he told her about buying the delivery basket and letting Shawn use his bike for his paper route.

"I've been taking the bus in the morning," Kareem explained. "It's annoying and slower than my bike . . . but at least Shawn is always on time for first period now."

"Well! I never thought my note would lead you on such an adventure," Teta said. "The name Kareem suits you."

"Thanks, Teta." He blushed.

"You know," Teta continued, "when you've gotten old like me, you realize the things you give away make you happier than the things you keep for yourself."

That made sense. Even though Kareem had worked all Ramadan to save up for his bike, he was actually kind of glad to be sharing it with Shawn. *Weird.*

"I have to hang up now, habibi," Teta said. "I don't want to burn my Eid basbousa. But I want to tell you something else before I forget."

"What is it, Teta?" he asked.

"Anytime you share something you love, it comes right back to you like a boomerang. You never lose it. Just wait and see."

✳ ✳ ✳

On Eid morning, the apartment smelled like butter, cinnamon, and coconut. No more fasting!

As Kareem put on his white thobe for Eid prayer, he heard a loud rapping at the door. "FedEx delivery!" a man called from outside.

"It's for me," Dad said, answering the door. "Wow, this is a huge box!"

Dad ripped open the note inside.

Dear Mr. Nasir,

Thanks for your fantastic work on the ad campaign. We look forward to working with you again. Enjoy this gift!

Yours truly,

OutStride Ltd.

"Shall we open it and see what's inside?"

"Yeah!" Kareem yelled.

Dad used kitchen scissors to slice open the layers of tape on the box before pulling out some Styrofoam padding.

Dad scratched his head. "It's a bike."

"Umm, Dad?" Kareem said. "This isn't just any bike. This is a Super Speedster X bike. It's exactly like the one I just bought. Like, *exactly* exactly. It's even the same color."

"Well, *that's* a strange coincidence," said Dad. "Anyway, I already have a great bike in storage. Since you inspired my design idea, the bike is yours."

There's no way this is a coincidence. This must be the boomerang Teta told me about. An Eid boomerang.

Kareem looked at the bike sitting in the middle of the living room. He immediately knew what he was going to do.

After Eid prayer, Kareem knocked on Shawn's door.

"Hey, Kareem!" Shawn said, yanking the door open. "Wait, wait—I know what to say today . . . Eed-moo-baw-rack," he read off his palm.

"Ha-ha, thanks," Kareem replied. "Eid Mubarak. Hey, do you want to go on a bike ride with me?"

"I know I'm skinny," said Shawn, "but I'm *not* sitting in the delivery basket."

Kareem burst out laughing. He grabbed Shawn's arm and pulled him into the hallway. Two identical shiny bikes stood there, waiting to be ridden.

"What . . . where did you get . . . I don't understand what's happening."

"It's a long story, and I'll explain it all. But first, get your helmet, and let's ride!"

The boys walked toward the elevator. A week ago, they had awkwardly stood in this same spot to go on Shawn's first paper route.

"This has honestly been the weirdest week of my life!" said Shawn, mounting his new bike outside their building.

"Same here," Kareem replied. "But a good kind of weird."

They both grinned.

As he rode next to his new friend, Kareem felt the cool breeze whoosh against his face. Teta's words echoed in his mind: *Anytime you share something you love, it comes right back to you.*

He believed it.

Don'ut Break Tradition

by S. K. Ali

It's Eid, but it doesn't feel like Eid.

    I'm wearing pajamas, the house is empty (except for Mama, who's sleeping), and if you look around and check in with all your senses, there's nothing to tell you today's a special day.

No delicious smells coming from the kitchen, no colorful balloon bundles in room corners, no music playing from the stereo system.

There's no happiness in the air.

I want to go back to bed.

But I can't, because I'm waiting for Mama to wake up and need me.

What makes a day special? What I mean is, what makes a *special* day special?

Today just feels like a day I don't have to go to school because my parents said so.

Because they *told* me it's a *special* day.

But so far it's been the opposite—an un-special day. Which is worse than a regular, normal day, when you think about it.

Tons worse, because my brain shows me all the things I should be doing today. The things we did every Eid before happiness left the house.

My bed calls me to climb back into it, so I force

myself to go to the bathroom to wash my face and brush my teeth.

I can try to pretend it's a boring regular day, at least.

I look at myself in the bathroom mirror.

Maybe it's because I'm wearing pajamas, not fancy Eid clothes.

Maybe that's why my face looks exactly the way I feel inside. Like all of me is getting squished and pushed into a small empty space I didn't know was there.

I *can* wear last year's Eid clothes from when I was ten. I still fit into the dress. Except for the way the sleeves don't reach all the way to my wrists.

And okay, when I tried it on yesterday, the neck was pinchy.

But last year's velvet dress is my favorite color— almost-black purple—and I know exactly where to find the dark tights that match it. (In the suitcase by the solarium window.)

But I don't change into Eid clothes.

Instead I check on Mama (still sleeping), pull on jeans, put on a coat, and run out of the house.

Because all of a sudden, I remembered something *special*.

Really special.

Donuts.

The donuts at Mr. Laidlaw's Bakery aren't like other donuts. That's what people say to each other. "Laidlaw's donuts? They're not like other donuts."

The next sentence is different for different people.

"They're fluffier."

"They're flakier."

"They're lighter."

"They're spongier."

And then my dad: "They're mystical."

I open the door to the bakery and join the line, which ends right in front of the entrance.

Morning rush. So many people sniffing the deliciousness in the air.

It *almost* smells like Eid.

When I'm third from the counter, I can see the entire selection of donuts. But my eyes go straight to my favorite at the very bottom right of the glass display case: the plainest one. So plain they're called Old Tyme.

"Yes?" It's the bored-looking cashier letting me know it's my turn. Her hair is striped pastel pink, violet, and gray and braided so that you can see each color separately. She has on four choker necklaces that go almost all the way up to where her neck meets her jawline. And she has on lipstick in my favorite purple-black color, but her face is like my favorite donut: no expression.

"Hi. I'd like six donuts," I say. "Apple Crunch, Cinnamon Swirl, Chocolate Chocolate, Strawberry Kiss, Powdered Delight, and Old Tyme."

"Half a dozen." She punches it in. "Coffee with that?"

"No. Just the donuts."

"It's free. It's a promotion. Buy half a dozen, get a coffee."

"But I don't drink coffee."

"Hot chocolate? Lemonade?" She indicates the display board behind her head.

"Um, okay. I'll have the hot chocolate." I hold out a twenty-dollar bill.

"You're Kareem's sister, right?"

"Yes?"

"I used to go to school with him," she says, a small smile lighting up her face.

Then it becomes big enough to show her braces, dark blue rubber bands on the top teeth and turquoise on the bottom.

Now her face matches the name tag on her uniform: *Joy*.

I smile back.

Can a smile make a day special?

Then her face switches back to normal, back to Old Tyme, and she hands me my change, a big turquoise ring flashing on her thumb.

Mama's sleeping face, her bare head resting on the pillow, flashes in my mind.

I count the change. Joy's given me an idea. And maybe I have enough money for it.

I walk back home, balancing the box of donuts in one hand and the cup of hot chocolate in the other, a plastic Buyway bag hanging off my wrist.

That's when I see him.

Mr. Laidlaw. In front of his own bakery.

He's coming out of a black car, hunched over and reaching for the cane that a younger man in dark glasses holds out for him.

I stop. It's like seeing Willy Wonka from *Charlie and the Chocolate Factory*.

But a Willy Wonka who you got to see a lot before he disappeared. Well, before he retired.

Mr. Laidlaw straightens and turns by holding on to the open car door. He has on a long black coat.

I realize I'm staring, so I begin walking again, head down, eyes on the slushes of melted snow still left on the ground.

"Hello there, I see you've bought my donuts." His voice sounds the same, just a bit quieter.

I stop and smile up at him. "Yes. They're for my family. For Eid."

He takes a step closer, and from beneath his short-brimmed black felt hat, his eyes peer at me. "Ah, yes. I remember your family. You'd pick up things for the mosque bake sales sometimes. And every Eid, you'd stop by on the way to prayers to get donuts."

I nod. Kareem's laughing voice comes into my head: *Don'ut* ever *break Eid tradition.*

"Your brother or sister would run in. And I'd see your mother on those bake sale days." His eyes are staring past me at the front window of his bakery. "I remember that she usually bought cinnamon buns for the mosque."

He looks kind of sad. Is it because he doesn't have a family of his own? Everyone knows that Mr. Laidlaw only has the bakery. Maybe that's why he visits it still—because it's like his family.

He turns to me again. "And you—I only ever saw you attached to your mother's side. You're Nadia."

"I'd always wait in the car on Eid."

"And now you're old enough to run in by yourself!" Mr. Laidlaw laughs, slow and rumbly. "Tell your family I said hello. And happy Eid. Where are they?"

He turns around to look at the road. To check for our car.

"They're at Eid prayers already. I stayed home."

"Ah, you're bringing donuts for them. How lovely, Nadia." He smiles in a kind way.

So kind it makes me blurt, "My mother is sick, and it's my turn to stay with her."

I don't add how sick.

I don't add what's in the plastic bag dangling from my wrist.

But if I look at his smile any longer, I might blurt everything out. "I have to go because she might be waking up now. Bye, Mr. Laidlaw!"

Mr. Laidlaw nods.

I used to love our house so much. It's red brick with wide steps leading up to an even wider porch.

It's hard to love it so much now that we live only on the first floor. We used to live in all of it, but then we had to rent the upstairs and basement out. That was after we sold the car. When happiness began to leave our home.

But every time something "bad" happened, Dad pointed out something good. Like that the bus stop is *right* outside our house. Actually, the bus heading south stops right outside, but the one heading north stops across the street. That's what Kareem told Dad with a laugh. Then he'd added, still laughing, *I know, I know, Dad! You're trying to tell us it's still pretty easy to go anywhere we want to go! Because, bus!* (Kareem's donut is Strawberry Kiss. Because he's like summer all the time.)

Early this morning, everyone hopped on the north-bound bus in their most beautiful Eid clothes from last year and went to Eid prayers.

Could it be that they took Eid with them when they got on that bus?

Before they left, Dad gave me my Eidhi, my money gift. "Because, binti, Daddy won't see you in the prayer hall to give it to you after salaat."

Twenty dollars.

"Why so much? Can you afford it?" I held the bill in my hand, in the air between us. I calculated. That was eighty dollars of Eidhi in total between all four of us kids.

"Yes, binti, I can afford it." Dad dabbed oud on his wrists and then wiped them on both sides of his neck, as he did every time he went to the mosque. The air filled with perfume. Dad's oud.

Mama's oud is still in the little glass bottle on the dresser. *Her* perfume has a bit of jasmine scent, her favorite flower.

After setting the box of donuts, hot chocolate, and bag on the porch to get my key out, I let myself into the house, pick everything up again, and go straight to Mama's dresser to get the jasmine perfume.

Eid doesn't only have to smell good because of food.

When Mama got sick, Dad began to work from home. He does people's taxes and accounts. He loves February, March, and April the best because that's when he has a lot of work. He calls it Happy Tax Crunch Time! (Dad's donut: Apple Crunch.)

Maybe that's why he can afford to give us each a twenty for Eidhi this year. Because it's February. Happy Tax Crunch Time.

Well, except that I don't have twenty dollars anymore. Now I have two dollars left.

I open the Buyway bag and look inside.

Mama's still sleeping. Beside her on the cream bedspread lie a dark blue abaya with big turquoise flowers on the hem, a navy cardigan, and her favorite slippers. Yes, they're fuzzy and worn, but they're also dotted with tiny pearly beads.

Noor helped get everything ready and spread the clothes out way before I even woke up this morning. But she'd whispered about it to me last night. *I want Mama to get ready for Eid day.* (Noor's donut: Chocolate Chocolate. Doubly sweet.)

For some reason, Noor forgot to put Mama's hijab on the bed too. I saw that this morning right after everyone left for Eid prayers.

Maybe it's because Noor has a lot on her mind now that Mama's sick and because she's the oldest.

Or maybe she thinks Mama doesn't need a hijab. Because of her hair situation.

But Mama loves her hijabs. She always loved wearing them to the mosque in Ramadan and on Eid. Before.

She had a *lot* of colorful scarves.

So I went through her things and looked everywhere, but there were only two hijabs left in her dresser drawer. Black and white.

Nothing special.

I set Mama's jasmine perfume and the Buyway bag on the kitchen table by the box of donuts and the hot chocolate that isn't hot anymore. I'd better get dressed first. If Mama sees me all ready, she'll probably want to change too.

Noor and I share the solarium room. Every morning, we pull the blinds up all the way on all six windows to let the light in. But then it feels weird getting dressed in there. It feels like the trees outside can see too much.

I change into my dress in the bathroom and leave the top part of the back zipper unzipped so my neck thanks me. Back in the solarium, I climb onto our bed to see the whole of myself in Noor's dresser mirror.

It's better than pajamas. I'll never ever get tired of purple-black.

I remember the girl with the dark lips at Mr. Laidlaw's bakery: Joy.

Plain, no expression, but still special.

I spot Noor's makeup bag on top of the dresser. *She isn't here to check on me.*

Noor doesn't have any dark purple lipstick, so first I put on dark pink. Then I put light red on top of that. Then I add some blue eyeliner and a bit of black eyeliner— but not on my eyes. On my lips. I smudge them in and smack them.

I climb back on the bed.

They kind of look like Joy's lips. And they almost match the dress.

They almost look special.

✳ ✳ ✳

After I help Mama use the bathroom, she eats watery oatmeal in bed with me sitting beside her.

I wonder if I should tell her about the donuts. I want it to be a surprise, but it was never a surprise *before*. We always just knew we'd stop for donuts on Eid mornings.

Don'ut ever *break Eid tradition.*

But still, it feels different today. Everything's different. Our house, our clothes, our Eid.

Then Mama looks up from her oatmeal spoon, and her eyes go from my dress to my lips.

Her eyes widen, and they look like they did before she got sick.

They look like they want to see *everything* again.

Everything in front of her and even more than that.

She smiles at my lips, covered in my favorite color. At first her smile is small, like a spark you're not sure you saw, but then it grows big—big enough for me to know something for 100 percent sure: *Yes, a smile can make a day special.*

I run out of the bedroom and into the kitchen. I put the jasmine oud and the Buyway bag and even the cup of hot chocolate on top of the box of donuts.

I carry it all like a tray to Mama and Dad's room that used to be Dad's office. Mama needs to know *everything*.

✳ ✳ ✳

But first, she needs to feel the way I do in my dress, in purple-black.

Leaving the things on Dad's desk, I get the clothes that Noor laid out on the bed.

Mama changes slowly. And I wait to help her only when she needs it. She doesn't need it that much.

Except when she looks in the mirror. I stand beside her and look in the mirror at her face, and it looks just like my face did before I ran out of the house this morning.

Squished.

I know she doesn't see anything special.

What makes a day special?

Smiles. Favorite-colored dresses and fancy lips.

And smells.

I unscrew the jasmine oud and hold out the wet perfume wand. Mama reaches her wrists out to get them dabbed and then rubs them together, but she never stops looking at her reflection, at the top of her bare head.

Her hair is growing in, but only in small bits, mostly only at the back.

"Mama? Do you want a hijab?"

"It's in the drawer, sweetie. The bottom right."

I open the Buyway bag. "Do you want your favorite color? Turquoise?"

It's a pashmina scarf, the kind of long scarf that's rectangular and soft and sort of thick. The kind of scarf that Mama used to wrap around her neck when she went to work, with her heeled boots and shiny black hair.

Now she can wrap the pashmina around her head, make her mouth smile, make her eyes wide, make herself feel special.

When she turns to me, her face tells me it's true—she's starting to feel *it*.

Like me.

We look at the donuts together. And I whisper to Mama, "Don'ut break Eid tradition."

Cinnamon Swirl Mama laughs, and it's like a door opens for happiness to step back into the house.

A door opens in me too, and I tumble out unsquished.

Mama lets me fix the scarf on her, and I pin it carefully under her chin. She looks beautiful.

"Why don't you drink your hot chocolate, sweetie?" she asks. "And have your donut?"

"No, I want to wait for everyone else," I say. "Do you think it will feel exactly like Eid did before? If I wait for them with a box of donuts? Outside?"

She hugs me all of a sudden. It's almost as tight as her hugs used to be.

"Eid Mubarak, my precious one," Mama says into my hair. "Now go outside to wait. Drink your hot chocolate so you can stay warm in the cold air."

"But they'll see me. And Esa might get mad that he didn't get hot chocolate too. Well, I mean *warm* chocolate," I say. "He might not even be happy that I got his favorite donut, Powdered Delight. You know how he gets, Mama."

"I have an idea! I'll make *everyone* hot chocolate." Mama begins walking to the kitchen.

"But, Mama, you can't!" I follow her. "You're supposed to rest!"

"Sweetie, I can boil water and stir chocolate powder. And I can see you, and you can see me through the kitchen window. I'll be right at the stove."

"But what if you get weak?" I move in front of her and touch her arms. "Like that day? Like last time?"

"I was doing something silly then, darling. I was trying to do the laundry." She holds my arms. "We'll keep an eye on each other. Through the window. Okay?"

Her eyes are wide. They're happy.

So I let her.

✳ ✳ ✳

I sip the warm chocolate sitting on the porch steps. They're so wide that Dad says it's like an extra sofa.

I smile. Now I get it. It's because we had to cut our living room in half with bookshelves to make a bedroom for Esa and Kareem.

So Dad's saying the porch is part of our living room now.

We're lucky to have such a porch.

The bus is coming!

I slurp the last bit of chocolate and tuck the cup behind the porch post. I don't want Esa to see it.

After picking up the donut box, I turn to wave at Mama, who I can see through the big kitchen window, stirring in front of the stove. Her turquoise-framed face smiles at me.

I don't think anyone will believe it's Mama standing there when they get off the bus. Well, maybe sitting there, because I pulled up a chair for her by the stove to rest on in between stirring.

With the donut box in my hand, I go only as far as the spot where our pathway meets the sidewalk.

They get off the bus. Kareem, Noor, Dad holding Esa.

And then more people get off the bus in front of our house.

S. K. ALI

I lower the box of six donuts.

Our friends: Aunty Zareena and Uncle Fawaz and their daughter, my best mosque friend, Hina. Uncle Ashraf and Aunty Mona and their boys, Kareem's friends, Talal and Munir. Aunty Hajera with her daughter, Firdows, Esa's best frenemy. And Mama's oldest friend, Aunty Rachel, with her daughter, Rebecca, who's like a sister to Noor.

I lower the box of six donuts even more.

"Why do you look like a vampire, Naddy? Your lips are scary!" Esa says to me when Dad sets him down. "Donuts? I want donuts!"

"Is that Mama?" Noor exclaims. "Why is she in the kitchen?"

"Eid Mubarak, Nadia!" Kareem opens his arms for a hug.

I let him hug me, I let Dad take the box of donuts for Esa, and I smile at Hina when Kareem lets go.

The bus speeds away.

Parked across the street is a black car. A familiar man in dark glasses leans against its hood.

I turn to look at the crosswalk in front of the bus stop.

It *is* Mr. Laidlaw making his way across to our house. With Joy beside him, holding a *big* box of donuts.

Enough for everyone!

"I couldn't believe it when Joy told me your daughter hadn't picked one of our special Eid donuts," Mr. Laidlaw tells Dad. "The new Cinnamon Chai donut. We've

74

been experimenting for a while and just put out our first batches this week. So of course I had to bring some over."

"What I can't believe is that Nadia even went to the bakery on her own. To keep up the tradition." Dad strokes my hair and smiles. "Come inside, Mr. Laidlaw. You must."

"I'd like that," Mr. Laidlaw says, stepping with his cane onto the pathway to our house. Joy has already followed Kareem onto the porch, where Noor's setting mugs of hot chocolate on the wide railing for our guests, some of whom are already sitting on the porch steps–sofa. Mama isn't at the kitchen window anymore. She must be sitting with her friends.

Now I know something I never ever want to forget, like I don't ever want to forget to love purple-black: *Special days start when you run toward them.*

So I run into the house, to the rest of this most special day.

Just Like Chest Armor

by Candice Montgomery

I t's beige.

Mama always corrects me and calls it "Tuscan Earth toned. With a touch of mauve."

I prefer just *beige*. It's easier.

Papí always takes my side. "Simple is good, querida. I like beige too."

The point is, I super like the way it looks against my cocoa skin, which I get from Papí's Caribbean roots. My skin, Papí always says, is dipped in sepia.

"With a touch of ochre!" Mama always adds.

But seriously, whatever the color, I love my scarf.

My hijab.

"Eleven is old enough, Mama," I say, trying hard not to seem like my goal is to talk her into something. It's probably not working. I don't so much roll my eyes as push them around my head in a large circular shape.

Which is totally different.

She walks around the kitchen island, swiping a gentle hand through my coarse hair as she goes. I've wanted to wear hijab for so long and have been begging and begging and begging Mama to let me.

The way I figure it, eleven years old is for real old enough. Eight was old enough for some of the other girls I know from masjid, but it wasn't until I turned eleven last month that Eima Ali gave me my first one as a birthday gift.

I like to think she was sending me a sorta secret message. *Get ready—it's almost time for you.*

It's no-holds-barred now. I wanted to take off running with that beautiful thing wrapped around my head six times the second I was able. But Mama. There was Mama, as always.

"Leila. Patience," she says. "Let me teach you to put it on before we jump in headfirst."

"*Head*first? A pun? Mama. Are you making a pun? Are you trying to take over as Silly Mama?"

She makes a face that says, *I am large. I contain multitudes.* But her job is being Serious Mama. Papí is the one who makes jokes, and he would never allow her to take his throne as family comedian.

"I wasn't," she says.

I knew it! "The rules are, you have to stick to Serious Mama."

"But," she laughs, "maybe I can be Silly Mama sometimes."

Papí walks into the den. A moment later, he pulls the scarf from my hands and wraps it around his shoulders like a cape.

"Papí!" I say. Papí is six feet six inches tall. He is a tree. I turn to Mama, hoping maybe she'll get my scarf down from his very high-up shoulders the way a fireman would rescue a lost cat.

No way I'm getting it down, I know. But I try anyway because that's just who I am.

Mama only stares at me. "You're probably right, honey. Best I stick to Serious Mama."

I let out a growl and take a running leap from the couch onto Papí's back, Tarzan style!

Papí has me in his arms, turned upside down, and then plopped onto the couch in a quick tornado of movement. But!

The good news!

I got it. I scurry to the other end of the couch, away from Papí, and cradle my scarf, brushing its softness against my chin.

The look on Mama's face is unreadable. She's got her bottom lip tucked in her mouth, and her eyebrows hang just a little lower than usual on her forehead. It's not sadness—not really.

Is "openness" an emotion?

"Oh, my sweet girl," she says.

I refold the scarf in my lap. "What?"

She shakes her head and then says on an exhale, "I love the way you love things. Let's do this, then. Let's get you in hijab, huh?"

And even though Mama doesn't like it, even though I know she'll hiss, "Simmer, Leila," the way she does, I stand on the couch and can't help myself—I do a little dance.

With a puff of laughter, Papí sits on the arm of the couch and says, "Well, if you don't want to wear it on your head, at least now we know it'll make a good cape."

Fiiiiiinally, Mama and Eima Ali decide to sit down with me and my beige-mauve scarf. It feels like a secret, the three of us in Papí and Mama's room, two scarves and a handful of pins laid out.

Mama has an entire drawer dedicated to her scarves. I think it's kind of like how mine has a special place on my shelf. Only, Mama has dozens. Blue ones and pink ones and silk ones and square ones and long long long ones and ones where the blue blends into the pink like watercolor paint and goes kind of purpley.

"Pick one," Mama says, and I glance up at her from my spot in front of her low dresser.

"What?"

"If you want to save yours for something special, you can have one of mine and we can teach you using that." She runs a hand over the top of my head, my chunky thick curls fighting with her fingers.

I like my scarf. I like Mama's scarves too, but I think putting this first memory onto my beige-mauve scarf would be really cool.

"Mm, can we use mine?"

Eima Ali smiles from her spot on the bed. Mama's hand squeezes my shoulder.

"Absolutely," she says.

"You know," Eima Ali says, "your mama and I used to race sometimes, in the mornings before school or before masjid. Who could get her hijab on the fastest."

I think Mama and Eima Ali have always been competitive. I'm a little like that now. "Who would win?"

Eima Ali stands proudly. "Me."

"Yes, your eima would win, but while hers were quickly done, pins clamped all wild and messy, mine always looked the cleanest, neatest," Serious Mama says. She is a pigeon, chest puffed and proud.

"You took your time so it would look proper," I say.

Mama nods and goes to sit criss-cross-applesauce on her bed. I join her. "It means different things to different people, but to me, having it look reverent—do you know what *reverent* means?"

I nod. "It's when you're super, like, respectful? And humble." Yeah.

She continues with the softest smile on her face. "Having it look reverent meant a lot to me. No one else besides Allah and me needed to get that."

I tilt my chin in understanding.

All of it feels like a thing you could write about. It feels special like that. And I will. Later I'll sit down and write some big story about the magic of a group of girls putting on hijab and fighting moon monsters and evil space beings.

Eima Ali brushes my hair back.

"You're not complaining that it hurts, Leila. Now I know your theatrics with *me* are entirely false," Mama says.

"No." I shake my head at Mama. "It's just that Eima Ali is softer. And she puts a lot of cream in before she brushes."

Eima Ali turns my head back in the direction she needs it. "Keep still."

"Mm," Mama says.

My halo of lightening curls is pinned back under the strictest orders to stay still and not move. And Eima places a thin black scarf around the edges and ties it in back.

"This is to protect your hair. We wear hijab, but that doesn't mean we forget the value of our hair. We still have to take just as much care."

Then, standing in front of the long mirror right next to Mama's perfume table, we start. And it's the coolest thing ever, pretty much. And I was right. It is a secret. Mama and Eima Ali teach me to wrap *diagonal* first and how to pin it in safe ways. And their voices are soft and slow the whole time.

Before Mama lets me look at the finished product in the mirror, she says, "There are a lot of ways to show our faith and love to Allah subhanahu wa ta'ala. You pick the ones that are right for who you are right now."

When I get to see things all finished and in place, I don't know how to keep my smile from leaping off my face. The way the softness feels around my cheeks, my chin. The way the beige-mauve-but-actually-just-beige looks with my skin.

"Papí!" I yell. And he comes running like there's a fire, coming to an abrupt stop just inside the doorway.

"Querida," he says, so quiet I almost don't hear him even though he's on his knees in front of me. And I don't know what it is about having Papí look at me with such pride, but I know right then that there are very few feelings that will ever top this.

He pulls his phone out and snaps a picture of the two of us together. Mama always says I stole Papí's smile right off his face for my own. She's right.

Papí, Mama, Eima, and I take *so* many pictures that we've all got sore cheeks by the time we're done.

I'm not allowed to leave the house in hijab right away.

Every morning I ask, and every morning Papí says, "Give it some time, querida. Mama's right. Just give it some time before we take off with it."

Now, with the sun kinda going down and all my homework done, I think it's probably a good time to ask again. So I do.

Mama glances up at me. "Get comfortable in it, sweet girl. There are a lot of different ways to wear it. Play around with some styles. Give yourself some time, and when you're ready, we'll order you some more." And then she goes back to prepping dinner, chopped onions flying all around the kitchen, ready to be part of dolma qarnoun tonight.

That weekend my best friend, Carmendee, comes over pretty much only so she can have some of the cassava pudding Papí made.

I like Carmen because she's super funny and because she likes Sailor Moon and cassava pudding and she never falls asleep early when we do sleepovers.

"Can I see?" she says.

"Duh! It's in my room."

"Hi, Mr. and Mrs. Aimé!" she calls as we hold hands and fast-walk through the house—because Mama's favorite phrase to yell is "Walking feet!"—and upstairs to my room, where my scarf has a special spot. Right on my shelf, next to my Sailor Moon collection. I've got the playing cards, the *original* dolls, the original and Crystal versions of the DVDs, plus the movies and Funkos, and then of course there's my manga.

Carmendee sits next to me on the floor in front of my mirror as I put on the hijab, and she helps me put the safety pins in where I tell her they should go.

"Dude, you could totally be the next Tahereh Mafi!" she says, scrolling to Tahereh's Insta.

Oh, man. I can dream. "Pretty sure I'm too dark to be, like, a mini Tahereh."

Carmendee laughs. "Oh, my God, 'too dark'? That's not even a thing. Your style's already super good. You dress like a rock star every day at school—even Michaiah said so."

Michaiah is a sixth grader who basically wears something from Hollister every day at school. No way am I on that level.

I laugh and swipe Carmendee's words aside—*poof!*— disappearing them forever. "All my clothes are from the segunda."

"Mine are too," Carmendee says. "But my mamí totally picks mine out. So it's kind of different."

That's fair. Mama always lets me do my own thing. Like, to an extent. Mama is still a pretty traditional hijabi with some super-strong Algerian roots, so I don't leave the house in anything outrageous.

"You should wear it to school tomorrow," Carmendee says, petting it the way she pets her dog, Taco.

Instead of letting me wear it out, Mama helps me

practice putting it on every day until I can do it myself. I only get more and more excited with every try, but I also get the feeling Mama's preparing *herself* for when I get to run free with it.

But . . . for Eid, maybe Mama will make an exception. Maybe Mama will let me wear it. I laugh before saying, "Want to do a TikTok to 'Sucker'? I love the Jonas Brothers."

We spend the afternoon filming and posting videos and talking about Nick Jonas, and I dance around my room with a little hopeful excitement in my hips.

In the coming days, I make it a goal to see just how many spots in the house I can wear it. In the kitchen. In the bathroom. In the upstairs closet. In the downstairs closet. In the storage shed in the backyard. Even in the garage, where I *never* go because seriously *who even knows* what kinds of bugs live in there.

After that, I approach Mama again. She's on the couch writing down her grocery list for Eid day dinner while Papí does tonight's dinner dishes in the kitchen.

"Well, now it knows where we live," I say.

She glances up at me for, like, a second. "What's that, my girl?"

I shake my scarf at her. "I've worn it around, shown it our house and also the backyard, the shed, and the garage. It knows where we live."

Papí yells, "Like *MTV Cribs!*" from the kitchen, and Mama snaps her fingers and says, "Jack Aimé, do not encourage her."

I turn and see him smiling into the bowl he's drying with a dish towel.

"Like, a baby's crib?" I ask, confused.

Papí barks out a laugh, and Mama shakes her head.

"Please, Mama? Please can I wear it? I want to wear it Eid day; wouldn't that be so cool?"

"Salaat. You'll wear it to salaat, okay?"

I frown. Wear it to masjid? *Only* inside the masjid? "No, but how 'bout all day, Mama? At school."

She says quickly, "No. That's not—I worry. The first time wearing hijab in public spaces can be . . . overwhelming and—"

If I let her keep going, I'll lose this battle of wills. "But Eid—that feels like a good time to wear it out for the first time. That feels right for me."

Like Papí always says, *I've got her on the ropes!* So I keep going. "I want to wear it Eid day because it's the way I want to express *my* relationship with Allah."

"Leila," she says.

"Got her on the ropes," Papí mumbles.

"Mama. Please."

And then Mama exhales. I smile.

Normally we go to Eid prayers every year, but this year's different because both Mama and Papí have work responsibilities they can't put off. Still, we pray Fajr in the morning together, and then we get ready. And I feel a little more bounce in my step than usual as I do.

My favorite part of putting on the hijab before school is the way Papí helps brush my chunky-thick curls back into a bun. He always sings under his breath as he brushes and puts in the hair butter.

Chunky-thick curls. My girlie's got chunky-thick curls.

Papí brushes much softer than Eima Ali, who brushes fast and firm, a little yanky here and there. But that's still not as bad as the way Mama does it.

Every "Mama, ouch!" usually gets me a "Mm, shhh, almost done."

And she is never. Almost. Done.

So Papí's hands in my hair feel like an okay way to start what Mama has *alwaysssss* said is "a rite of passage." To wear hijab out of the house and in spaces that test who we are.

When I get out of the car that morning, Mama says, "I love you. Eid Mubarak, sweet girl."

"Love you too. Khair Mubarak, Mama." And I don't *mean* to slam the car door shut, but excitement makes my hands heavy.

I give one last wave and then heft my backpack a little higher, feeling the coolness vibes of my whole outfit come together.

Black jeans, leather jacket, and, yep—hijab. Steady. Ready. *Beige*. In place and prepped to go.

Except it's different than I thought. People look at me, but they don't really *say* anything. I know I won't be able to see Carmendee until after lunch because I'm in class A and she's in class B, but I kinda expected some of my other friends, like maybe Jupiter or Aja or Yuki or Keturah, to be a little excited.

I'm sitting at my desk, writing in my morning journal about it. About how Kyle from class D yelled, "What's on your head?" when I walked by this morning and I pretended not to hear. About how I kinda get why Mama wanted me to take my time with it. About how I'm not sure what it means if I don't want to wear hijab after today.

I'm done journaling and start drawing a Chibiusa doodle in the corner of the page when my seatmate, Tennyson Korpi, plops his empty-sounding backpack onto our table.

"Hi, Leila," he says. To me his voice always sounds like when you eat cherry shaved ice too fast. Soft, but also kinda sharp somehow?

"Hi," I say back.

I can see out of the corner of my eye that he hasn't sat down yet, so I glance up at him as he says, "I like your, um," and then gestures around his own head in a weird way.

"Thanks—it's called hijab."

"Cool," he says. "Oh, hey. Eid Mubarak! I put the day in my phone's calendar when you mentioned it last month."

"You did?"

He sits. "Yeah! And then I went on Google and looked up a little bit about it and, like, how to say the right stuff to you."

I feel my nose crinkle in that embarrassing way when I ask, "Why?"

He shrugs. "I don't know." He says it all quiet, and I think maybe I shouldn't have asked him that.

Tennyson has been my seatmate since, like, fourth grade. He's always been way nicer to me than anyone else, and at the beginning of the year, when Mrs. Holcomb asked if we wanted to sit next to each other again this year, Ten and I both said yes, but when *I* said yes, my chest got all hot and my heart started to beat really fast, and when I got home I asked Papí what heartburn was, except it wasn't that.

Ten's started writing in his own morning journal, but when he notices I've stopped drawing he says, "What? What's wrong?"

I shrug like I don't know, but *I do know*. "I feel kind of weird wearing hijab today. Which, like, is probably what my mom was talking about when she told me to wait."

"Oh."

That's it. That's all he says. Till he leans back in his chair, the front two legs tipping up off the ground. "Why do you feel weird? Is it uncomfortable?"

"No."

"It smells really nice."

"Oh. Thanks?"

He coughs and then says, "Is it because Kyle Broadbeck yelled that thing on the playground this morning?"

"Yeah, kinda. Also because no one's saying anything nice. Except you. They're not saying anything at all, so it makes me feel like they're saying bad stuff about it instead. And at my mosque we learn that it's super not about what other people think. We learn that it's about what we think and what Allah thinks. And I just expected to feel a little different. More, like, full, I guess? I don't know. I expected to feel the way I always feel on Eid day."

"How do you feel normally?"

Pretty good question. "Happy? And, like, really excited for every part of the day because it means that I'll get to go home and go to masjid and see my friends there and then have dinner with some of them and their families."

"That sounds kind of nice."

"It is! It's *so* nice."

Ten nods. "So, how you're feeling now—do you not still feel happy and excited for those things?"

Mrs. Holcomb stands up from her desk and hums the first five notes of "Shave and a Haircut," and the rest of the class, seated at their own tables, sings the rest of the line back, signaling the start of class.

I hadn't really thought about it. Probably because Kyle Broadbeck yelled and knocked all my happiness vibes right out the nearest window. But I think maybe that's the point.

Maybe . . . maybe we wear hijab even knowing that the Kyle Broadbecks of the world will yell at us from across the playground and make us feel small. And so then it's our job to look to Allah SWT to guide us back to that place of grace and pre-Kyle happiness.

I run my hand along the side of my head and smile.

Mrs. Holcomb asks who wants to read their morning journal to the class. Ten and a few other people raise their hands, but she picks Maisie Mannon. When Maisie is up in front of the class reading, Ten slides his journal over to me.

I can't really read his handwriting, but I catch some of the big pieces.

He wrote about me. Ten wrote about Eid and so also pretty much about me.

Today is Eid day for Leila and a bunch of other people who practice Islam.

Super glad Leila is my seatmate and my friend because she smells like strawberries all the time, which is pretty cool, and she teaches me things I never knew.

List of People I'd Like to Learn Stuff From:

- *Leila*
- *Anthony*
- *Nala*
- *Manuela*

And the list goes on for, like, ten more names. I laugh quietly, imagining Ten up there reading names of, like, basically half the class.

I bump his shoulder with mine, and when he looks at me, I mouth, "Thank you."

He nods.

Maybe there's some stuff I can learn from Tennyson too.

Mrs. Holcomb is asking Tatiana Pijot to read next. Tati starts reading the lyrics of a song she wrote about loving tacos.

Same, Tati. Same.

I flip a page in my journal and start drawing another doodle. This time it's one of a magical girl in hijab with her magical sun powers and her sun scepter and her faith, which she wears as chest armor.

Gifts

by Rukhsana Khan

Hmmm. If I were an Eid gift, where would I hide? Under the bed? Too obvious.

Near the furnace? Nope.

I squeeze past Sulaymaan to check behind the sofa. Dust bunnies.

Sulaymaan says, "Just leave it, man! Wait till Eid like everyone else."

"How can you be like that? Aren't you itching to find out?"

Sulaymaan looks up from the Quran he's reading. "Well, yeah. But we've got a whole month to get through, and Ramadan is about a lot more than just gifts."

He doesn't want to admit how much he likes getting gifts too.

The leather couch lets out a *booff* sound as I flop down on it. I kind of like the noise, but Sulaymaan looks over at me like I did something wrong, then goes back to reading.

His lips move, and I can tell he's not just reading the English translation—he's doing the Arabic too, even though it's harder. And something about him irritates the heck out of me. So I toss a cushion at him.

"Quit it!" he says, and pushes the cushion behind him. He doesn't even toss it back.

There's so much time to fill when you're not eating or drinking!

Right on cue, my stomach rumbles. Suhoor was a long time ago.

I say a bit too loud, "Why do we even have to fast?"

Sulaymaan puts down the book and looks at me like I'm dumb. I thought he'd be glad for the chance to lecture me.

"It's only my second year," I add.

"Well, it's kind of like thanking Allah for the gift of guidance. The Quran first came down in Ramadan."

"But why do we fast?"

He looks thoughtful. "I think it's a reboot. A sort of training."

"Huh?"

"If we can be strong enough to resist the stuff Allah has allowed, it makes it easier to resist the stuff that's forbidden. I know Ramadan makes me appreciate the things He gave us that I usually take for granted, like food and water."

He's back to reading his Quran. I can't help but think of the pictures I've seen of starving kids in Yemen, and I feel ashamed.

It's hard having an older brother who's better than me.

The sun's getting ready to set.

Its rays light up the clouds on the horizon, so they

glow around the edges like an inspirational poster. The traffic is quiet on our street. There's only one guy out walking his dog.

I close my eyes and listen to the birds calling to each other as they return to their nests for the night. I wonder if they're saying, "See you tomorrow!" "Good night!"

Mom calls, "Idrees, it's almost time to break."

When I come inside, she asks, "How was your fast?"

Then she and Dad and Sulaymaan stare at me, waiting for me to answer. I hate being the youngest. They never ask Sulaymaan!

"Piece of cake!"

Sulaymaan laughs. "You had a piece of cake?"

"No! I mean—"

He looks shocked. "Idrees! You can't eat cake while you're fasting! Don't you know that?"

"I didn't!"

"Was it chocolate or vanilla?"

Dad and Mom laugh too, and I feel so dumb.

Mom brings out the Ramadan boxes. It's a tradition she started a few years ago, something she saw on Instagram: thirty small boxes containing some candy and a hadith or Quranic ayah for each day of Ramadan. She offers it to Sulaymaan, but he waves it toward me and says in a Moses–from–*The Ten Commandments* voice, "You don't have to bribe *me* to fast!" Then he points at me. "Let the *child* have his *bonbons*!"

Dad looks confused. "Bonbons?"

"Candy," says Mom, and they both laugh. But then Dad looks at me and tells Sulaymaan, "Stop teasing your brother."

I say, "You don't need to bribe me either!"

Mom pats the side of my face. "Oh, honey. It's not a bribe. It's encouragement!"

"I'm eleven!"

Mom pinches my cheek. "Too old for candy? Fine! *I'll* have them!"

And she pops the Jolly Ranchers and Nerds into her mouth, and I have to look like I'm okay with it. Grrr.

Sulaymaan reaches over and reads the little slip of paper from the box out loud. "God said: 'Every deed a person does will receive ten to seven hundred times reward, except fasting, for it is for Me, and I shall reward it. There are two occasions of joy for one who fasts: one when he breaks the fast, and the other when he will meet his Lord.'"

Are they looking at me again? It sure feels like it.

It's a school night, so we pray Taraweeh at home.

As if Isha isn't long enough, we have to pray eight extra rakats. Dad and Sulaymaan take turns leading. Behind us, Mom closes her eyes and smiles just before we begin. She looks so peaceful in her hijab and long dress.

I don't groan out loud when we start. I don't dare. But I swear it feels like the prayer will never end.

But it does.

Eventually it always ends.

As we're getting up from the last rakat, Dad rubs my head and gives me a quick hug. "You want to lead tomorrow?"

"Sure!" I say, and again I feel ashamed of the way I was feeling.

Mom takes off her hijab and is folding it neatly when I catch her off guard by asking, "Um, did you buy the Eid gifts yet?"

In the way she glances quickly at Dad and says, "Never you mind," I have my answer.

I'll have to double my efforts!

While I'm snuggling into bed, it feels like the month will last forever, and yet the first day of Ramadan is already gone—one thirtieth is already done. One step closer to Eid.

Basketball practice is hard while I'm fasting! I'm panting like I never do, and my best friend, Liam, says, "Not even water?"

"Nope."

"That's hard!"

"Yeah." Right now it is.

I wipe the sweat from my forehead, and as I pass by the water fountain, I take a mouthful just to rinse out the dryness.

But there's something about the water swishing over my tongue. It's only water, but it tastes so good! The urge to swallow is strong. Nobody would ever know. When I was young, I wouldn't have hesitated, but now . . . I spit it out.

It wasn't easy.

So why am I smiling as I head to class?

Mom didn't hide the gifts in the laundry room.

And they're not in any of the closets either.

When it's time to break my fast, I plop down in my seat harder than usual.

"Are you all right?" Mom asks.

"Fine! Just fine!"

She hunts through a bunch of dates and picks out the fattest, juiciest one. "Here."

And she hands me a glass of water. The date is so sweet that it makes the spots just behind my jaw tingle, and the water is colder than from the fountain.

I feel better.

I'm standing at the kitchen sink drinking another cup

when I notice the moon high in the sky. It's big, like a cookie with a huge bite taken out of it.

Mmmm, cookies!

I'm just brushing off the cookie crumbs when Dad calls. It's time for Isha.

And when we begin the Taraweeh, I step forward to the prayer mat at the head of them all.

Sulaymaan, with his *Ten Commandments* voice again, says, "Don't forget, you're leading all our prayers!"

Dad says, "Leave him alone. He knows."

I do my best to concentrate and not let my mind wander. There's no need for Dad or Sulaymaan to correct me, and when I'm done, I step back so Dad can lead. Mom gives me a thumbs-up, and Sulaymaan can't say anything.

Tucked into my bed later, I think, *That's the second fast done—one-fifteenth of the month over.*

The third night I think, *That's one-tenth*, and after the fifth day, all of a sudden, it's one-sixth.

On the seventh night, me and Sulaymaan are on the porch drinking mango juice, watching the moon rise long after the sun has set. It's half full.

"Okay, smarty-pants, why do we use the moon to tell time?" I ask him. "Why can't we just use the regular calendar so Ramadan is always at the same time of year?"

Sulaymaan says, "All ancient societies used the moon

to tell time. The Native Americans, the Chinese, the Jews, the Hindus, and lots of others."

"So, the month is a quarter done?"

"Yup."

"It's so pretty."

"Yup."

Just then a breeze springs up and flutters my hair. Along with the taste of mango juice, it feels perfect.

On the weekend, we go to the masjid for Iftaar and Taraweeh. Mom turns to me. "Don't let anyone distract you. Remember what you're here for!"

"Yes, Mom." She never tells Sulaymaan that.

The hall is packed with a lot of Muslims who only come during Ramadan. I know people who don't follow most of the stuff, but when it comes to Ramadan, they go all in. There's something about fasting as a community.

The rows are awfully close together, and when the prayer begins, I end up squished between Sulaymaan and a man with a bushy mustache and big belly.

Even though the imam who's reciting has a beautiful voice, it's hard to concentrate because the man beside me keeps quietly burping. After a day of rest, his stomach is going *gurgle, gurgle, gurgle*.

The imam says, "Allahu Akbar." And we have to go down on the floor for sujood.

BONK!

With the rows so close together, I guess a head-to-butt collision was inevitable. My head, the guy in front of me's butt.

I must not laugh! I must not! But when Sulaymaan starts giggling, I do too. We've ruined our prayer.

We both break it and start again. We'll have to make up the ruined rakats.

By the ninth day of Ramadan, I'm kind of tired. As soon as I come home, I drop my backpack on the floor in the hall, and before I can stop myself, I say, "I miss eating during the day."

Mom rushes over. "You feeling all right?"

"Yeah! Just tired."

"Don't fast tomorrow. Take a break. You're still young."

So I do, but then there's all the questions at school—"Why are you eating?" "Did you forget?"—and the looks from the other Muslim boys who are still fasting make me feel guilty.

Before I know it, the day is done, and the feeling of watching Mom and Dad and Sulaymaan at the dinner table choosing their dates and insisting that I have one too, even though I didn't fast, feels so awkward.

After Taraweeh Dad asks if I want to skip another day. "No. Wake me for suhoor."

Mom says, "You sure you're up to it?"

"Yes!"

And I am. The day passes easily.

When I have my date to break my fast, it feels like I really deserve it.

I still haven't found the gifts. Every year I try and fail to find them. I wanted this year to be different.

It's while I'm praying Asr that it finally hits me—the one place I didn't think to look! As soon as I'm done, I check if the coast is clear.

Mom's busy in the kitchen.

I slip into the garage. She always leaves her car unlocked. I open the driver's-side door and press the button for the trunk. *Click*.

My heart's in my throat as I come around the side of the car, and there it is. Nestled in her trunk. The Ultrasonic Super Revved Drone with HD camera in red, my favorite color.

It's great!

Perfect!

So why do I feel so flat?

What's wrong with me?

It's exactly what I wanted.

I should pick it up, right? Make sure the box is real, heavy.

It is.

Should I open it?

Nah. It's not Eid yet.

And then I see the brand-new hoverboard that Sulaymaan has been wanting.

But I don't bother picking that up.

I put the drone box back where I found it, trying to place it exactly so she won't know I've been here. And I sigh, I actually sigh, as I'm closing the trunk. What's wrong with me?

When I come into the kitchen, one look at my face and Mom says, "You found it, didn't you?"

What should I say? Will she yell?

While I'm thinking how to answer, she shrugs ever so slightly and turns away. "Well, I hope you're happy."

"Mom, I'm sorry."

She looks up, surprised. "No, no. It's okay. It's just that now you know. There's no surprise, is there?"

And I guess just to show me that she really doesn't have any hard feelings, she messes up my hair and gives me a shove. "Go and water the garden, will you?"

I do, without complaining.

✳ ✳ ✳

It feels weird knowing that I'm getting exactly what I wanted.

What's the word? Not sure.

Not disappointed exactly—I can't wait to show my friends—and yet . . .

I throw myself into the little things to make up for it.

And I do extra chores to earn money so I can buy my own Eid gifts for them.

You can tell when the moon's really full when it appears opposite the sun in the east just as the sun is setting in the west.

Ramadan is half over!

It went so fast.

And now the moon starts to wane. Every night it gets a little smaller, rising a little later. Tonight it doesn't show up till we're on our way home from Taraweeh. It's three-quarters full.

The last ten nights!

Now the heavy worship really kicks in and we go for Taraweeh every night.

I stand next to Dad and Sulaymaan, feeling grateful for more than the drone in the trunk of Mom's car.

I don't know what's happened, but it's like I can rise above the congregation, a God's-eye view, and see all of us bowing and prostrating as one, and I can feel deep in my bones all the gifts, the things that have gone right in my life, starting with my parents and Sulaymaan.

I need to buy their gifts.

"Can you drive me?" I ask Sulaymaan the next day.

"Why do you always wait till the last minute?"

I shrug.

"I've got exams. Ask Mom."

So Mom drives me, but the problem is that she follows so close behind me in the mall. When I walk faster, she does too till I turn on her. "Mom! I need some privacy."

"But I don't want anyone to snatch you!"

Argh!

I guess she sees my frustration, because she sits down on a bench beside a bushy plant and says, "I'll just wait here while you do your shopping, okay?"

Yes!

I get Sulaymaan's gift from a sports store.

I find cologne for Dad and a nice hand cream that smells like roses for Mom. I can picture the smile on Mom's face as she puts it on in the morning and then catches its scent throughout the day.

Just as I'm about to check out, Mom sees me and rushes over. "Let me take a look-see."

And before I can stop her, she opens the bag with the elbow and knee pads. "For Sulaymaan, right?" And she picks up the cologne in the basket, takes off the lid, and sniffs. "Ooh, your dad will love this!" But then she frowns. "Who's the rose cream for?"

"Mom!!!"

"Oops!"

I turn to go find her something else, but she puts a hand on my arm and stops me.

"Don't put it back."

"But—"

"I like it. Don't put it back."

So it stays.

And from the way Mom goes about the rest of her day with a smile on her face, I wonder if ruining the surprise really mattered.

And when I ask her, she says, "Oh, Idrees, it's never about the gift. It's about the love behind it." She pulls me close and rubs my head. "It's sweet that you think of me with roses."

Does that mean she thinks of me as a flying drone and Sulaymaan as a hoverboard rolling along the ground?

Hmm.

Sounds about right.

During the last few nights of Ramadan, the moon whittles away and disappears, or at least we can't see it.

We're on the porch under the moonless sky, drinking more mango juice. The month is almost over. I'm going to miss it.

I ask Sulaymaan, "Isn't there a saying about appreciating things when they're gone?"

He nods. "You don't know what you've got till it's gone."

Yeah. That's it.

When it's finally Eid and Mom hands me the box wrapped up neatly and tied with a bow, I pass her my gift, less neat with no bow. I wrapped it as well as I could.

Dad likes his cologne. If I didn't know better, I'd swear by the way Mom squeals that she didn't know what she was getting.

I watch Sulaymaan's face as he tries to open my gift to him. It's entombed in duct tape.

"Argh!" he says, and goes to fetch some scissors. But I hid them. So he tries to get a knife, but I hid all of those too.

We all laugh as my super-dignified older brother has to bite and pry and tear at the package.

When he finally gets it open, the knee and elbow pads fall out. He grins at me, and I realize Mom's right.

It's not the gift.

It's the love behind it.

The Feast of Sacrifice

by Hena Khan

I grab my duffel bag and am about to leave my bedroom when I spot an envelope sitting on top of my faded checkered bedspread. It's addressed to me.

I can tell it's from my mother even before opening it. The kiss mark in pink lipstick is a dead giveaway.

"Dear Humza," Mama's distinct sloping handwriting says. "I just want you to know we love you so much and are so proud of you."

Mama must not have been satisfied with our hurried goodbye this morning. I wasn't about to let her kiss me a hundred times and squeeze me while she cried and held up the middle school drop-off lane. So I gave her a quick hug and jumped out of the minivan before anyone saw us.

"Please pray hard over these next two weeks. Ask Allah to accept our Hajj . . ." the letter continues.

For the past few months, my parents have been preparing for the Hajj pilgrimage—a once-in-a-lifetime journey to Mecca. Baba actually started going to the gym to get in shape. They went to special classes to learn what it would be like and bought things like cooling towels and collapsible water bottles. Somehow, even after their suitcases were packed and the day had arrived, it still didn't feel like they were actually going. Maybe that's because I didn't want them to leave.

". . . and please pray that Allah brings us back to you."

I gulp as I read that part. I watched videos of Hajj with my younger sister and brother to learn about what our parents would be doing. We saw footage of millions of pilgrims crowded into the city of Mecca. They were dressed in simple clothes, walking the paths of the prophets who came before us, remembering, performing rituals, and praying. It's hard to imagine my parents there, even if it means they get to do something they've dreamt of for years. What if something happens to them? What if they get sick? Or hurt by the crowds? Or . . . worse? I push the thoughts out of my head and read on.

"Please be a good boy and take care of Ayla and Ismail. You mean the world to them, and they need you. And please help Nani and Nana Abu take care of you. We're counting on you and can't do this without you."

Usually I'm glad when my parents leave us for an hour or two and I'm in charge of Ayla and Ismail. I control the TV remote, call dibs on my favorite snacks, and get to be the boss. But twelve days? I didn't sign up for this. That's too long for a twelve-year-old to be the boss, whether they're counting on me or not. Plus, we're staying with my grandparents, which means I'm going to have to do a million chores. They've always got a list of things for me to do whenever I come over. I scan the rest of the letter with blurry vision as the weight of my parents being so far away for so long hits me and my eyes start to fill up.

"I miss you so much already. See you soon, Insha'Allah." Mama signs off with a bunch of Xs and Os. And I have to admit, I wish she were still here to give me real hugs and kisses right now instead of leaving us and flying across the world. I tuck the letter into my pocket, pick up my bag, and head downstairs to where my grandmother is waiting to take us to her house.

The TV is blasting a Pakistani news channel that my nana Abu is watching in the family room while I try to concentrate on my homework. I'm sitting on a formal dining room chair, stiff and covered with fancy fabric like most of the furniture in my grandparents' house. Somehow it feels dark even though it's sunny outside, but we're not allowed to turn on the lights or waste electricity until Nani closes the thick satiny curtains that hang from the windows.

I helped Ismail with his second-grade math worksheet, and now he and Ayla are playing in the backyard as I struggle to get through my own work. Nani can't edit my personal narrative essay like my dad would, and Nana Abu doesn't explain seventh-grade algebra as well as Mama does, even if he is a wizard at crossword puzzles.

"Come, Humza, set the table," Nani calls from the kitchen. "Tell Ayla and Ismail to come in and wash hands. Let's eat."

I glance outside and see Ismail poking in the dirt with a stick and Ayla juggling a soccer ball and telling him what to do. We've been here for three days and so far they haven't been fighting as much as I expected, but Ayla's been whining a lot, and Ismail is quicker to cry than usual. They act so helpless that I have to step in and help them make their lunches and do their laundry. That's on top of all the stuff my grandparents ask me to do, like sweep out the garage and put boxes into the crawl space, since Nana Abu can't lift heavy things anymore.

I make Ayla help me set the table and tell Ismail to fill the water pitcher, and then we sit down together in the kitchen, my stomach growling. I load heaps of rice, chicken, and some spiced yellow lentils onto my plate and dig in. I've already devoured half my food when Nani notices Ismail quietly picking out all the onions and making a pile of them on his plate.

"What are you doing?" she asks. Nani's gray-and-black hair is pulled back into a bun, and the lines on her face that are usually smiling are helping to form a frown.

"I don't like onions," Ismail says.

"Oh, sorry, I forgot. Next time I grind them, okay?"

Nani helps him pick out the rest and then notices Ayla, who is poking at her chicken with her fork.

"Why aren't you eating?" she asks.

"I don't like chicken with bones," Ayla says.

"Take it off the bone, then," Nana Abu suggests from across the table. He's wearing a thick blue sweater with brown buttons and slippers and is sitting so straight he looks younger than seventy-five, even though he moves slowly and has trouble hearing sometimes.

Ayla flips a chicken leg over with her fork, her round eyes bugging out of her head more than usual. When she makes a gagging sound, Nani takes her plate and starts to pull the meat off the bone for her. I look at Ayla as her eyes grow glassy and wonder if she's thinking about how Mama never forgets what everyone likes and doesn't like.

Nana Abu clears his throat.

"You know Eid-ul-Adha is coming soon, right?"

I forgot that the holiday was going to happen while my parents were away. We talked about that a long time ago, but now it hits me. This is going to be the first Eid we've ever had without them.

"This Eid honors the story of the prophet Ibrahim and his son," Nana Abu continues. "He was ready to sacrifice his own son, but God in his mercy performed a miracle and replaced the boy with a goat."

"Wasn't it a sheep?" Ismail interrupts. "My Sunday school teacher said it was a sheep."

"Goat, sheep—that isn't the point. Now we remember that event on Eid and how we should be unselfish and willing to make sacrifices. That's why we sacrifice an animal and share the meat with the community, right?"

Ismail looks at me with a confused expression. Ayla takes the tiniest bite of chicken and chews.

"I'm going to be a vegetarian," she declares.

"No, no, no." Nana Abu shakes his head. "You should be grateful for the blessing and gift of being able to afford meat. When I was growing up, we were lucky to have it once a week. Do you understand?"

"I don't even want meat. Or chicken. Mama and Baba said I can be a vegetarian when I turn ten if I want."

Nana Abu looks at Nani for help but she shrugs. I sort of understand what my grandfather is saying about being grateful, but I don't feel it that much right now. Plus I have no idea how to explain it to a picky nine-year-old, so I quietly finish off the rest of her chicken when I'm done with mine.

"You need to help Nani with the dishes," I order Ayla a few days later.

"I did it last time," Ayla argues. "It's Ismail's turn."

"She asked *you* to do it," I remind her. I've been doing

so much, and there's no way she's going to keep getting away with watching TV all afternoon.

"Why do I have to do it? She asks me to do more than Ismail. Is it because I'm a girl? Because that's not fair."

"You're older than him. And it's not because you're a girl. I do way more than both of you. I've been doing everything since we got here."

"You can't make me." Ayla stomps her foot.

"You better do it, or you'll be in trouble." I turn back to the game I was playing on my phone. It's the one thing that's been keeping me from losing it. My parents have been gone for less than half their trip, but I am so ready for them to be back. I know it's a lot for my grandparents to watch us and that I'm supposed to help them out, but it feels like whenever I sit down to relax, I get assigned another task.

My phone buzzes in my hand. It's Mama calling on WhatsApp.

"It's Mama!" I yell, causing Ismail to drop his action figure and run over to me. Ayla shoves him out of the way to get closer to the phone.

"Stop it!" Ismail says, pushing her into me.

"Both of you, stop," I command while I connect the call. A grainy Mama fills the screen.

"Assalamu Alaikum, guys!" Her face lights up, and I smile back.

"Salaam, Mama. How are you?"

"Salaam, Mama," Ismail and Ayla chime in.

"We're doing fine, thank God. We're in Medina right now, and it's so amazing. Look at this mosque."

Mama walks around and shows us the columns and gold-and-black arches, and she points out the details on the carpet and the lights.

"It's so beautiful and peaceful here. And there are people from everywhere in the world—I've met the nicest women from Malaysia, Sudan, Argentina, and Sweden. It's incredible, and I wish you could be here with me."

"I do too," I say.

My mother is wearing a gray hijab tied tight around her face and a flowing abaya instead of her usual jeans and shirt, but it's not just the way she's dressed that makes her seem different. She looks so happy it's like her face is glowing.

"How are you guys? I miss you so much," she says.

"We're okay." I swallow hard. "We miss you too."

"Are you being good?"

"Yeah."

"Ismail hits me and doesn't listen." Ayla sticks her face in front of mine. "And Humza's being bossy."

"I did not!" Ismail yells.

"Ayla is giving Nani a hard time and not helping." I glare at Ayla.

"You guys." Mama's face clouds. "Please? Please, can you get along? I need you to behave."

Ayla and Ismail start to sniffle.

"Please? I know it's hard, but it's how you are helping Baba and me so we can do this, right? So we don't have to worry about you?"

"Fine," Ayla concedes. "I guess we can . . . *sacrifice*."

"Well, okay, then." Mama laughs. "That's a big new word. I like it. Thank you for that."

"You don't have to worry about us," I add, giving Ayla and Ismail a warning look.

"Thank you." Mama's face is shining again. "We leave for Mecca from here to actually start Hajj, so it will be harder to be in touch, but we'll call again soon."

"We love you," I say.

"Love you!" Ayla and Ismail add.

Mama blows us a kiss and wipes her eyes, and then she's gone. I didn't get to tell her I scored a goal in my game yesterday. Or that I made pancakes this morning and that they turned out almost as good as hers.

"You need to wash the dishes," I tell Ayla.

"Fine." Ayla keeps her promise to Mama and drags herself over to the sink. "Ismail, you have to help."

I sigh. Keeping my own promise to be nice while I'm in charge has been harder than I imagined. I try to remember that peaceful look on my mom's face as I realize we still have a week to go.

✳ ✳ ✳

"What is *that*?" Ayla covers her mouth in horror as she walks into the kitchen, where I'm grinding onions, and spies the mound of bones and meat on the counter.

"This is goat, the meat Nana Abu got from the butcher for our Qurbani," Nani says. Her sleeves are rolled up, and she's wearing a stained apron.

"Qurbani?" Ayla asks.

"The animal we sacrifice for Eid. Remember we talked about it?" Nani explains. "Eid is in two days."

Ayla turns and looks at me, utter disgust on her face, and whispers, "I'm so going to be a vegetarian."

I'm almost tempted to join her as the onions make my eyes water and we watch Nani slice fat off chunks of meat.

"Can I stop now?" Ismail is peeling the skins off garlic cloves, standing on a step stool so he can reach the counter.

"How many do you have?" Nani asks.

"Seven."

"I need twenty."

"Are you really cooking all of this?" I ask as I stick another onion in the food processor. "It's so much." I've seen my grandmother put out a feast for a party before. But this is a monumental amount of meat.

"We're taking it to the mosque on Eid for everybody to eat."

"What else are we doing on Eid?" Ayla asks as she laces up her sneakers by the garage door. Her friend's mom is coming to pick her up for soccer practice.

"We'll go to the masjid for prayer. Distribute the food to everyone who comes for lunch. Then we'll come home."

"Wait. That's it?" Ayla's mouth falls open. "Aren't we going to parties?"

"Parties? Maybe we'll visit our friends. But don't worry, there will be so many Hajj parties when your parents come home, Insha'Allah."

Ayla looks at me in alarm. Eid is usually a whirlwind, starting with prayers at the mosque, snacks, and bounce houses at the carnival, then lunch with our grandparents, and then at least two or three parties. We eat dessert all day long, see most of our friends, and get tons of presents and money. What's this Eid going to be like without our parents *or* any parties?

"Don't worry, Eid will be wonderful," Nana Abu says as he walks into the room.

"Is the rest of my garlic ready?" Nani asks.

I give Ayla a sympathetic nod as she opens the door. I know she is wishing our parents were going to be home for Eid as much as I am. Because I'm pretty sure our grandparents' idea of wonderful is really different from ours.

"Eid Mubarak! How are you, sweetie?" One of Mama's friends moves toward me through the dense crowd on the lawn of the Islamic center. She's draped in a bright turquoise shawl, and her daughter, clutching her hand, is decked out in a glittery gold getup and matching cat ears. It's like a sea of colors as everyone moves around the lawn and greets each other with smiles, and the bronze dome of the mosque glints in the sunlight. Auntie gives me a big hug.

"Eid Mubarak, Auntie." I return to the station by the side of the community building, where I'm helping to ladle bowls of Nani's korma—the savory stew she cooked for more than five hours—and pass them out. We got here extra early, well before the first prayer, so we could set up the food in an outdoor kitchen area.

"How are your parents?" Auntie asks. "Did you talk to them today?"

"Not yet. But they texted and said they finished Hajj."

"Mubarak! You must be so proud."

"I am," I say, and I mean it. Last night before bed we all talked about the few things my parents still have to do before they leave, which include Baba shaving his head today. It's going to be so funny to see him when he gets home in two days.

"Do you want some?" I hold out a bowl of korma to Auntie.

"Is it spicy?" She hesitates to take it.

"Not too much. It's really good." I tasted it, and it's honestly the best I've ever had. Nani made sure to grind up the onions in the entire batch so Ismail wouldn't find a single one, and she cooked a small separate pot without bones for Ayla. We all agreed it was delicious, even the future vegetarian.

"Thank you." Auntie takes the bowl and a piece of naan.

As she dips the bread into the sauce and takes a bite, I watch her face transform.

"Oh my. This is incredible."

"I know." I've handed out at least thirty bowls so far, and it's been the same reaction each time. One man came back for three servings, and then he asked Nani for her recipe. She said she makes it with love but didn't reveal anything else. No one is getting her secret ingredients.

"Go play now, Humza." Nani comes up behind me and puts a hand on my back. "You've helped for a long time." I've been here for almost two hours, while Ayla and Ismail ran off to the bounce houses with their friends after about fifteen minutes.

"I'm okay," I say, surprised to hear myself say it. But it's been fun to hang out with my grandmother and her crew. They've been chatting, teasing each other, and making wisecracks all day, which reminds me of how I am with my best friends from Sunday school, Sami and Qasim. They stopped by earlier but already left for a party.

"Okay." Nani squeezes my shoulder, and I can tell she's pleased as she winks at me. "You're always a good helper, Masha'Allah."

"Eid Mubarak," an older auntie whose name I forgot says to us as she approaches. She slips me a five-dollar bill. "Eidhi for you."

I thank her and add it to the growing wad of cash in my pocket from all the Eidhi I've been collecting today. The auntie asks me about Mama and Baba, telling me how happy she is for them and how she's been praying for them. That's how it's been all day. Some people tell me their own Hajj stories. Others mention that my parents added their requests to a prayer notebook that they took with them, filled with the wishes of the community and our family. I've already heard of three Hajj parties planned for after they get home. It's awesome to see how much their trip means to our entire community.

"Here you go, Auntie." I hand her the last bowl of stew and then realize with a pang of regret that I didn't save any for myself. At least I got to try it at home last night.

Since we're done, Nani insists that I go rest, so I sit down on a bench and look around at the crowd, watching the mix of people, old and young, rich and not, speaking different languages and wearing their nicest clothes. There's a blend of colorful African prints, sparkling saris, leather kufis, and embroidered shalwar kameezes like mine. Everyone has happiness on their faces and is here for the same reason—to gather and feast and worship. It occurs to me that this is probably similar to what Mama described Hajj to be like, on a smaller scale. I hope I can make the pilgrimage one day too.

Nana Abu comes walking up with a bowl of korma and two pieces of naan.

"There you are. You worked hard. I saved this special bowl for us."

"Yes! You're the best!" I grin at him and say bismillah before tearing off a piece of the naan and scooping out a chunk of the meat. It's salty, spicy, and melts in my mouth.

Nana Abu's lips part into a smile through his short gray beard as he watches me. In the past couple of days, he went to the butcher shop twice, got all the groceries for Nani, and figured out how to pack up all the food in crates into his trunk. Nani was on her feet all day yesterday cooking the korma and had to lie down with a heating pad at night. Both of them spent hours of the holiday feeding a crowd of friends and strangers. But here's my grandfather, looking even happier than if he were sitting in someone's living room at a party.

"It's been a wonderful Eid so far, hasn't it?" Nana Abu has a little bit of stew and then wipes his mouth with a napkin as I dip into the korma for another bite, feeling full throughout my insides, including my heart. This morning he called this Eid the "feast of sacrifice," and I think I have a better idea of what that means now.

"Yeah, Nana Abu," I say. My grandfather holds up his phone and shows me a new photo of my parents in front of the Kaaba in Mecca. We laugh as he points out my dad's new haircut, and I feel a swell of joy. "It's actually been great."

Seraj Captures the Moon

by G. Willow Wilson

illustrated by Sara Alfageeh

Searching for Blue

by N. H. Senzai

Toes digging into the warm sand, Bassem stared out across the endless expanse of cobalt sea to the line where it met the sky, a gentle aquamarine. As he marveled at the incredible shifting shades of his favorite color, blue, a memory drifted back to him of a hot summer day like this one three years ago, when he'd been nine years old. He and Babba, his father, had been picking golden apricots in his grandparents' garden.

"Did you know," Babba had said, as he began a lot of his conversations when he wanted to impart some tidbit of knowledge, "that many ancient cultures didn't have a word for the color blue?"

The fact had confounded Bassem. "How can that be?"

Babba, an ophthalmologist who was fascinated by all things related to sight, smiled. "You see, blue doesn't appear much in nature. There are few blue animals or foods, and blue eyes are pretty rare. If you read ancient texts in Sanskrit, Chinese, Hebrew, or Arabic, there is no word for blue. It's as if people back then couldn't recognize the color."

"What about the sky?" Bassem had asked. "And the oceans?"

"An ancient poem about a sailor lost at sea, written nearly three thousand years ago, described the ocean as a 'wine-red sea,'" said Babba. "No mention of the word *blue* in the entire book. And besides, are you sure what you are seeing *is* blue? Many would say the sky and the ocean are colorless, white, or gray."

Bassem had craned his neck back, noticing that the sky, close to dusk, was white and pale yellow streaked with pink and orange.

"Habibi," Babba had said, "always look beyond what your eyes initially recognize and find out what is real, what is possible, and what is the truth."

Now, as Bassem stood on the shore of the small Greek island, all he could see were the white-capped waves that had nearly taken his life. More than a month ago, in the dark of night, he and twenty-eight others had set sail from the Turkish coast. The water had been a thick, oily black, waiting to engulf them as they sat crammed inside a vessel designed for fifteen. Every minute of the crossing had filled Bassem with gut-wrenching fear, though he hadn't let it show. Confidently, he'd held on to Ummi, his mother, and his little sister, Dina, eyes probing the sea, looking for land. Forty minutes later, waterlogged and freezing, they'd crawled onto an island. They'd huddled in shock, with nothing to their names except a few small bags. The suitcases had been tossed into the sea to lighten the load.

A deep rumbling in his stomach soon interrupted Bassem's bleak thoughts. Hunger was a familiar sensation, developed over years of living in a war zone. But for the past month, the hunger had been in observance of Ramadan. He sighed. Babba had loved the holy month of Ramadan, when you abstained, from dawn to dusk, not only from food and drink but also from negative thoughts and actions. It was a time of reflection, personal improvement, and increased devotion to God. It was also a month of charity, and Babba had always made sure they'd shared their blessings with others less fortunate than they were.

Babba. Bassem's gut twisted as he remembered his father coming home from his eye clinic, pockets full of candy for him and Dina. Bassem would never see him again, and he felt empty, parched of emotion. Even the anger that had burned in him like a hot ember had eventually crumbled to ash, gray and devoid of possibilities.

"B-Bassem," stuttered a voice from behind him, interrupting his dark thoughts. It was Dina, heading up to the beach, half a dozen of her friends in tow. "You p-p-promised to p-play!"

Bassem sighed. His peace and quiet were gone. They'd found his hideaway, a good distance away from the tourists tanning along the beach, enjoying their vacation. He pulled a plastic bag out of the scuffed-up duffel bag that he carried around. Inside were a dozen glittering marbles, procured in a trade that morning.

"You g-got them!" said Dina. Her stutter had developed as the bombings had grown in number and ferocity. When she got anxious or excited, it got worse.

Bassem nodded. "Let's go," he said, watching the kids' faces light up. He led them across the beach toward the main road that separated the sea from the quaint, whitewashed buildings of the small town. Down the road, he spotted his cousin Rheem waving at him. She stood talking to a girl with short, sun-kissed hair.

He'd seen the girl a few times, either on the beach or dining with her family in the expensive restaurants lining the main street. Waving back, he moved on toward a picturesque port where fishermen unloaded the day's catch. Bassem gave them a friendly nod. He'd be back later to help mend their nets or clean their boats. He skirted past a tavern where the owner did not appreciate their sort. Bassem had learned that the hard way when he'd knocked on the door, looking for work.

"We don't want filthy, dirty refugees here," the red-faced owner had screamed. "You're ruining our island."

Bassem had apologized and beat a hasty retreat. He'd heard from the other refugees that people in Greece were already struggling to make money in a bad economy and didn't want others competing for the few jobs they had.

Solemn and peaceful, the Church of Mary rose at the corner beside a restaurant where octopus hung from pikes, drying before being grilled. The Apollo Hotel came next, a bright pink concoction resembling a fluffy birthday cake. A boy stood at the gates, sweeping the steps.

His eyes lit up when he saw Bassem. "Can you come by later?" he called out. "My mother needs help in the kitchen." His English was good, having grown up as the son of hoteliers catering to tourists. He also spoke German, some French, Italian, and Spanish. No Arabic though, so Bassem had to use his rusty English.

"Hey, Constantine," he replied. "Sure, I come in a few hours."

"Bring b-back some of his mom's cake," whispered Dina, an impish smile on her face.

Constantine's mother had been the first friendly face they'd encountered on the beach the terrible night they'd arrived. She and other islanders, along with a few tourists, had led them to the Apollo Hotel, where they'd received warm clothes and a hot meal, including a rich honey cake. They'd stayed until the volunteers from Helping Hands charity, Hussain and Emily, had arrived. Hussain, a college student from London, had been spending his summer working with refugees in Greece. He'd piled them into a rickety old van and driven them to the old tomato processing factory that would be their new home, established to accommodate the stream of refugees that had begun showing up that spring.

Bassem clenched his fists. Home. His heart tightened as he remembered his family's comfortable apartment in Syria, golden sunlight flowing through its many windows. He'd stood at the living room window and watched thousands of protestors march by, demanding freedom, equality, and a fair government. In response, President Assad had sent in rockets, bombs, and the military, turning Bassem's city into a battlefield. Then a graveyard.

Hussain soon became like a big brother to Bassem, helping him and his family navigate the legal spiderweb that would take them to Germany, where his uncles had found asylum. When Hussain had to return to university, the loss hit Bassem hard. Emily, the volunteer from Sydney, was great, but she wasn't as warm and gregarious as the Britisher. Bassem still kept in touch with Hussain using Ummi's cell phone, which he kept operational with his meager earnings. The cell phone was their lifeline to their uncles in Germany and family still in Syria and scattered across Turkey and Jordan.

The factory that was now their home stood beside a football pitch, encircled by a chain-link fence made colorful by the clothes drying along its length. Bassem and the other children slipped through the gate and walked past the supply shed, a logo for Helping Hands painted on its side. Inside the cavernous space, he found Ummi lying on a cot, her eyes closed. He was glad to see her resting, since sleep had deserted her upon leaving Syria. She was awake most nights, pacing or reading the Quran. In her hand she clutched one of the only things that had survived their flight—a wooden cookie mold that had once belonged to her great-grandmother. The family had made nut-filled ma'amoul cookies with it for more than three generations.

He and Dina headed toward their aunt, who stood near the makeshift kitchen that the refugees shared. "Habibi, did you find any work today?" she asked.

"I'm going to Constantine's to help in the kitchen," he said.

"You're such a good boy," she said, giving him a hug. "And can you believe it—it's the last fast today."

The words struck him like shrapnel, the sharp pieces of metal that rained down when bombs fell across Syria. "It's Eid-ul-Fitr tomorrow—Babba's favorite holiday," he murmured.

His aunt nodded sadly as Dina grabbed a snack of stale crackers for the other kids. "It's E-Eid?" she asked.

Bassem nodded, handing her the marbles. "Go play with them. I'll be with you in a few minutes." Dina was too young to remember the details of an Eid before the war started, but memories fluttered through Bassem's mind like fragments of iridescent tinsel—his grandparents' home filled with family and friends, stacks of presents and packets of money for the children. And the food . . . His mouth watered as he remembered the succulent kabobs, rich stews, mounds of jeweled rice, crispy roasted potatoes, and his mother's specialties, the sweets: honeyed baklava, towering cakes, luscious puddings, and cookies of more than a dozen varieties. The images faded from his mind. His grandparents' home was gone, reduced to rubble, his grandparents trapped inside.

A month after their last Eid together, Babba had sat them down on the sofa. "I am an ophthalmologist," he'd said, "an eye doctor who helps people see. But for years we have lived blindly under a government that is corrupt and evil. We have to open our eyes and look for a better future, even if we have to fight for it."

That night, Bassem's father, uncles, older cousins, and men from the neighborhood had joined the rebels fighting President Assad. And within a year, his family had received a text from Babba's younger brother, one they'd feared: Babba had been killed during a bombing raid. All around them, the country fell into terrible chaos. Bassem's uncle urged Ummi and his aunt to leave the country and made plans to meet in Germany. So as fast as they could, they'd collected more than six thousand dollars to pay smugglers to get them out of the country.

"Salaam Alaikum, sister," came a soft voice. It was Uncle Yakuba, an elderly Nigerian man who'd been at the factory when they'd arrived. The unelected head of the place, he provided sage advice, soothed frayed tempers, and led Friday prayers.

"Walaikum Assalam, Uncle," replied Bassem and his aunt.

"We will have Eid-ul-Fitr prayers tomorrow morning on the football field," said Uncle Yakuba. "I've spoken to others and they think it's a good idea."

Bassem blinked. Prayers. Prayers had gotten them nothing since the day the killings and destruction had begun.

"I agree," said Bassem's aunt. "We need a little bit of joy around this place."

"Masha'Allah, your nephew is a bright, hardworking young man." Uncle Yakuba smiled at Bassem, his teeth white against his cocoa-colored skin. "I will need your help."

"What time?" Bassem asked woodenly.

"Around eight, when the weather will be cooler. Then we can have a little something to eat."

"All right," said Bassem. "I will get the kids to help lay out sheets for prayer. But what should we do about food?"

Uncle Yakuba's smile faded a little.

"I'll check the shed," said Bassem's aunt. "There is rice, some lentils, and a lot of flour. Alhamdulillah, food to fill our bellies."

"We will make do," said Uncle Yakubu.

"I'll go tell the older kids to help," said Bassem, quickly walking away.

But instead of looking for Javaid and Amir, the two Afghan brothers his age, Bassem grabbed Ummi's cell phone and hurried toward the football field, avoiding Dina and her friends. He stumbled and collapsed beneath a flowering bush, huddled amid the vibrant pink flowers. Helplessness and doubt gripped his heart, and without warning hot tears ran down his face. This would be their first Eid without Babba, his grandparents, the rest of his family. There were no presents for the kids, no special foods to celebrate the end of a month of fasting and praying . . . prayers that continued to be unanswered. It was as if God had forgotten about them altogether. He shivered, trying to do as Babba had asked, to look beyond the terrible circumstances that had brought them here, but he just couldn't.

He didn't know how long he'd been sitting there when he noticed a pair of scuffed sneakers standing a polite distance away.

"Bassem," whispered a concerned voice. "Are you all right?" It was his cousin Rheem. Embarrassed, Bassem wiped his cheeks. "It's okay," Rheem said. "You can't always be the strong one. It's okay to let it out."

Bassem grimaced as he rose, mumbling, "It's Eid tomorrow."

"Yeah, I know." She sighed.

"Uncle Yakuba wants to have prayers on the football field in the morning," said Bassem.

"Well, that's important," said Rheem. "Though it will be a little boring—there's nothing special to do, especially for the little kids. No new clothes, gifts, games—nothing."

Bassem nodded, having thought the same thing.

"I wonder . . . does it have to be boring?" pondered Rheem. "Maybe we can get some balloons . . . and a cake or something."

Bassem blinked. "Cake?" he muttered.

"I know, I know . . . a cake big enough for everyone will be way expensive," sighed Rheem. "But somehow, we need to find a way to make this a good Eid."

Cake? thought Bassem as the wheels in his head started to spin. In his mind, he saw his mother holding the cookie mold. If they couldn't have a big fancy cake, they could have ka'ak cookies, simple circles of sugar, flour, and butter that his mother flavored with whatever was at hand. "Ka'ak," he burst out.

"Huh?" said Rheem.

"I'm going to get stuff for Ummi to make ka'ak," said Bassem.

"Ka'ak, cake, good one," laughed Rheem, eyes lighting up. "From where?"

"Don't worry about that," said Bassem.

"Okay, then I'll figure out a way to prepare games for the kids," said Rheem. "Silke can help."

"Who's Silke?" asked Bassem.

"She's the girl you saw this morning. Her family came for the holidays, but they extended their trip. They've been working with Helping Hands, seeing if their friends in Germany can help."

Bassem's heart lifted, and he spotted a glimmer of aquamarine beyond the gray cloud that had descended over him. Most tourists looked at refugees like them uncomfortably or pretended they weren't there, ruining their vacations. But others, like Silke's family, weren't like that; they saw them as human beings. As Bassem left the football field to grab his duffel bag, he made a mental note to send Hussain an Eid Mubarak message when he got to the hotel.

Constantine and his mother were busy in the hotel kitchen when Bassem arrived, sweaty and out of breath.

"Hello, Bassem," called out Constantine's mother as she stirred a pot of apricot jam.

"Hello, Kyria," replied Bassem, using the Greek term for *lady*, as he tucked his bag under the counter.

Constantine tossed him a bottle of cold water, for later, and grinned. Bassem smiled thankfully, tongue-tied for a moment. He shrugged off the self-consciousness and got to work unloading boxes of cereal and passing them to Constantine, who stacked them in the pantry.

It was later, after the work was complete, that Bassem found the words he needed. Constantine's mom was opening the cash box from which she usually paid him.

"Kyria," he began softly, "tomorrow is our celebration of Eid—the end of our holy month of fasting for God. Instead of euros, can you please give me something else?"

"Something else?" she asked, soft brown eyes confused.

"Yes," said Bassem. Then he explained what he needed. As he shared his plan, tears began to gather at the corners of her eyes.

Dawn arrived on a blessedly cool morning as Bassem and the older boys laid out the sheets for Eid prayers. His body was weary, but his heart light as he thought about the night before. He'd returned to the factory, duffel bag full of supplies. Instead of euros, Constantine's mother had given him butter, sugar, and spices. As soon as his mother had peered inside the bag, she'd crushed him into a hug and called everyone to her like a drill sergeant.

Soon the rickety oven was heating up while the ladies flew into action, measuring and mixing, while the kids were sent to search for anything that could serve as baking sheets. All activity ceased as the rich, buttery smell of ka'ak filled the factory. Everyone was given a crumbly disk to taste, flavored with anise and fennel, and as it melted on their tongues, Dina had shouted gleefully, "So this is what Eid tastes like!" The room had burst into laughter, and after carefully packing away the treats, they'd all fallen into a deep sleep, even Ummi.

Now, as the inhabitants of the factory awoke, the air was filled with a buzz of anticipation. Uncle Yakuba and the men set up tables on the grass, which would soon be laden with bread, feta cheese, lentil stew, and hot tea to be shared for a hot breakfast after prayers. Rheem, Amra, and the other girls were in another corner of the field, setting up a series of simple games for the kids. And somewhere near the shed, Ayoob, a shy Yemeni man, played his wooden flute, which always brought a sense of peace to everyone.

Slowly, with care and courtesy toward one another, the inhabitants of the factory formed lines facing east, toward the holy city of Mecca. Soulful and melodious, Uncle Yakuba's voice settled across the field, focusing their little community in prayer. As Bassem knelt, an ember rekindled in his heart, yearning for a connection with God. As they were finishing, a line of cars pulled up beside the field. To Bassem's surprise, he saw Constantine and his family. From the next car tumbled a group of fishermen and their wives. Half a dozen other islanders and tourists, including Silke and her family, came next. As they pulled packages from their vehicles, Emily drove up in the rickety van, bright balloons bobbing out the window.

The quiet of the morning broke as Constantine ran to Bassem and everyone shared greetings, shaking hands and hugging. The guests had brought fresh fruit, boiled eggs, and pastries, which they added to the table, creating a feast. Together they sat and ate, laughed and sang as Ayoob's flute played in harmony with one of the fishermen's guitars. With a warm smile, Ummi passed out ka'ak, filling everyone with the richness of Eid.

"Bassem, isn't this so great?" shrieked Dina as she ran by with her posse to Rheem, who was setting up a game of tug-of-war with Silke, who'd also created a station near them to paint the little ones' faces.

Bassem grinned and realized with surprise that her stutter had momentarily disappeared. Like him, she'd forgotten—forgotten that they were refugees far from home.

"Eid Mubarak." Emily strode toward him.

"Thank you so much for coming," said Bassem, "and for the balloons."

"Hussain sent me a message that it was Eid," she said. "And I have some good news," she added, smiling from ear to ear. "I heard from the main office in Athens."

"Really?" gulped Bassem.

"They are reviewing your papers to go to Germany," she said.

"We're going to Germany?" gasped Bassem.

"Don't get too excited so quickly," she advised. "There's still a lot to do, but it's a start."

Unbidden, Babba's voice echoed in his mind. *Always look beyond what your eyes initially recognize and discover what is real, what is possible, and what is the truth.* Perhaps God hadn't forgotten them after all. Hope filled Bassem's heart, and his eyes refocused, his sight suddenly flooded by the sky, a shimmering azure streaked with cobalt and hints of navy blue and ultramarine.

Creative Fixes

by Ashley Franklin

"W atch out!"

Makayla flinched as a basketball bounced off the table, next to where she was sitting.

She still found it odd, eating in the masjid's gymnasium, but the gymnasium also served as the dining hall during Ramadan and special occasions. Makayla returned her attention to her phone and continued scrolling through pages of dresses.

"Makayla! Makayla, are you even listening?" Amira whined.

Makayla didn't notice. It had finally happened. She'd found it—the one! The most perfect Eid dress! It was white with silver and gold embroidery around the bodice. It looked royal. It looked rich. It looked . . . like something her parents would never agree to spend so much money on. Still, a girl could dream. Makayla added it to her online shopping cart.

Amira playfully elbowed her friend in the arm. "I'm starting to think you're tired of listening to me talk."

"What? No!" Makayla waved her phone in the air. "You know . . . just . . . phone stuff."

"Prove it, then," said Amira. "What was I talking about?"

Makayla saw a number of eyes—a distressing amount of them, actually—all turn in her direction from both sides of the cafeteria-style table. Stuffed mouths—which had only a few minutes ago expressed how glad they were to finally be able to eat for Iftaar—stopped chewing.

"You're so extra." Makayla picked up a spoon. "You were talking about—" Makayla shoveled a giant spoonful of biryani into her mouth and mumbled.

"Nice try," Amira laughed, "but you're not getting out of it this easy."

Makayla's eyes began to water. She fought to hold back tears, but she couldn't. In her attempt to dodge Amira's question, she hadn't thought about the spiciness of the food.

She still wasn't used to it. Any of it, really—the spicy food, the fasting, the whole converting-to-Islam thing. These community dinners were doing more to bring out Makayla's anxiety than to bring her closer to the other girls at the masjid. Amira had been the only one to really reach out to her. Sure, Amira was a bit pushy, but Makayla wasn't in a position to be choosy when it came to friends.

Amira passed Makayla some raita. She tried not to laugh. "It's not even that hot! And that's what you get for trying to dodge my question."

At the moment, Makayla didn't care how right Amira needed to feel. All she knew was that she'd never been so excited to see yogurt in her entire life!

The eyes went back to their plates. The other girls were no longer interested in Makayla and Amira.

"Thanks." Makayla took several more scoops of raita to ease the raging fire that was happening in her mouth. "Your Eid outfit. You were talking about your Eid outfit."

Of course Makayla knew what Amira had been talking about. Amira's abaya had arrived weeks ago, and she hadn't stopped talking about it since. Makayla didn't think her friend was trying to be obnoxious. She was just excited. The dress was pretty. There was no doubt about it. It had been custom-made overseas and was covered with sequins and rhinestones in fancy patterns. Really, it was more than pretty. It reminded Makayla of some of the wedding dresses her aunt had circled in bridal magazines before she'd gotten married. Makayla didn't own anything so fancy. The fanciest thing she owned was the idea of wearing the abaya she'd saved to her shopping cart.

"Let me see!" Amira snatched the phone out of Makayla's hand.

"Quit playing!" Now Makayla was annoyed.

"Oh. So *this* is what you've been doing," Amira said more loudly than she needed to.

It worked. She'd captured the rest of the table's attention again. Amira turned the phone around so everyone could see its screen. A few of the girls inched closer for a better look.

"It's gorgeous! Don't you think?" Amira waited for the other girls to agree with her. They did, of course. "Is this your Eid outfit?" she asked Makayla.

Makayla snatched the phone back. "Well, no."

"Don't you like it?"

"Well, yeah."

"So why don't you buy it? It's already in your cart."

Because it was two hundred dollars. But Makayla was not about to announce to the whole table that her parents couldn't afford it. She'd eat fifty plates of mouth-burning biryani before that happened.

"Because it'll never get here in time. Shipping. You know." Makayla was proud of herself for coming up with such a logical answer on the spot. You couldn't argue with logic!

"I know!" Amira's eyes widened and her voice got higher. "It'll be my Eid gift to you! I'll pay for express shipping! My mom said I could pick a few friends to give Eid gifts to, and this is perfect." Amira reached in her purse and gave Makayla a gift card, the kind you could use anywhere.

"I—I couldn't." Each breath Makayla took felt heavier than the last. She focused on a boy dribbling a basketball just past their table and breathed deeply. Perfect. You couldn't argue with logic, but apparently, charity beat logic.

"Don't be silly," Amira giggled. "It's only a fifty-dollar gift card. And you deserve that dress. It's gorgeous."

Makayla gave Amira her biggest, phoniest smile and desperately turned all her attention back to her phone.

✳ ✳ ✳

Makayla's mom was not having it. "Give it back!"

"Mom! I can't give back an Eid gift." Makayla plopped down on the sofa.

"Fine," her mom said. "Then I'll give it back."

Without even looking up from her sewing, her mom had crushed Makayla's dreams. Makayla had spent all of last night thinking about how to tell her mom what had happened. She'd even let herself believe that her mom would let her get the dress after all so she wouldn't seem rude or unappreciative of Amira wanting to pay for rush shipping.

"Why keep that girl's money if it's for a dress you're not getting? That's selfish!"

Makayla crossed her arms and sucked her teeth. "It's selfish if I don't get the dress."

"Here, Bilal." Her mom passed Makayla's little brother the newly repaired pants whose patches he closely inspected before nodding his approval.

"End of discussion, Makayla! I already told you we're going out today to go Eid shopping."

"Great. More time together," Makayla mumbled.

"I can do without the attitude, miss," her mom said. She picked up Makayla's phone from the end table. "Tuh! Two hundred dollars for a dress." She shook her head. "That's a bill."

Makayla pouted.

Her mother placed the phone in her lap. "Get dressed."

Makayla, her mom, and Bilal hopped into "Big Sis"—their Toyota Corolla that was older than Makayla. The three of them had been spending more time together than usual over the past few days, cooking and decorating every inch of their tiny apartment to give it "a more Islamic feel," whatever that meant. Makayla's mom wanted everyone to feel special and included for their first Eid. Because of their efforts, homemade decorations filled their apartment—it was nearly impossible to find Eid decorations in stores. Eid was like their new Christmas, but without the bombardment of songs on the radio, the school parties, or the ugly sweaters. Now, thanks to her proud mother, Makayla couldn't even enjoy the one similarity that remained—gifts. Makayla knew her parents were trying their best to make their transition to Islam fun and exciting, but it was all a lot to take in. The spicy food, the different culture, the way they had to dress now, the things they had to give up (especially pepperoni pizza) . . . it was a little overwhelming.

They pulled up to a strip mall that they usually went to on Saturdays when the thrift store had its twenty-five-cent sales. They started at the end of the strip and worked their way through the stores. With each one, Makayla's mood lifted. She really liked the new plates and bowls they got from the dollar store for their Eid meal. They were purple and gold and reminded her of royalty.

At the thrift store, Makayla's mom found a plain white dress that fit Makayla perfectly. It wasn't fancy, but it was okay. Her mom even found a white dress for herself and a nice white shirt for Bilal. Dressing alike was something Makayla had loved about Christmas. It was something they'd done each year for their Christmas cards. Maybe Eid wouldn't be so bad after all. Makayla and her mom happily chatted as they left the thrift store while Bilal walked ahead of them, munching on a pretzel.

"Makayla! Girl, is that you?" It was Amira. She and a few other girls from the mosque were walking up the sidewalk with white trash bags.

Makayla had never seen them outside of the masjid. Why today? Why here? Why now? Makayla's lungs felt too big to fill up with the air she desperately needed. The bag with the plates and bowls slipped out of her hand. *CRASH!*

"MAKAYLA JACKSON, WHAT IS THE MATTER WITH YOU?!" Makayla's mom hurried to pick up the bag off the sidewalk.

"You here for sadaqa, too?" Amira didn't wait for an answer. "Our parents make us give away some of our stuff to the needy each year as part of our sadaqa. I guess that's cool because it's charity. But it's kind of weird thinking I might see someone walking around in one of my old outfits."

Makayla couldn't speak. She looked at the girls. She looked at Bilal. Makayla's pleading eyes met her mother's.

Mrs. Jackson sighed. "Makayla, why don't you and your brother relax in the car for a few? I might be a while in the fabric store." She dug the keys out of her purse and passed them to her daughter.

"Thanks, Mom." Makayla grabbed her little brother's hand and ran to the car.

"See you tonight at the masjid for Laylatul Jaa'izah!" Amira yelled after Makayla.

Makayla gave Amira a quick wave and a mumbled salaam without looking back. She and Bilal sat in the car for some time before their mother came out.

Mrs. Jackson didn't glance in Makayla's direction as she got into the car. "I raised you better than that," she said. It was that quiet, hurt tone that Makayla couldn't stand. She hated when her mother was disappointed in her. The ride home was extra long and extra quiet.

✳ ✳ ✳

It may have been her first Laylatul Jaa'izah, but Makayla was sure it wasn't supposed to feel like this. The gymnasium was packed with games, food, and fun. Everyone there was having a great time. She, on the other hand, was only having *a time*, replaying the afternoon's events over and over in her head. She looked down at her hands and arms. The henna she'd gotten was beautiful, but you could barely see it against her skin. More than anything, Makayla was starting to wish for Ramadan to come back or for Eid to hurry up and leave.

In fact, she wished things could go back to the way they were before they'd converted. Everything about her new life made her feel out of place.

Finally, they left the masjid, and Makayla climbed the familiar set of stairs that led to her family's apartment. She trailed behind her father, who was carrying an already-sleeping Bilal in his arms. Her mother had left the masjid early, saying she had a few last-minute things to do at home before Eid the next morning. The apartment was nearly dark. The tiny light on the sewing machine cast a small glow on her mother's garment bag. It was stretched across the sofa with bits of purple thread scattered about. Makayla ran her fingers across the bag, picturing her mother wearing the white dress that was inside. She wondered what purple "creative fixes" (as her mom called them) her mom had made to it. Maybe a fancy embellishment? She thought about her own white dress from the thrift store and frowned.

Tomorrow her friends at the masjid would know the truth. Her family didn't have a lot. They didn't have a fancy car. They sometimes ate beans and rice several times a week. Most of their clothes had patches or creative fixes sewn onto them. Unless the night before Eid was something like the night before Christmas in so many stories she'd heard growing up, Makayla was sure there wasn't going to be any miracle that would get her the dress she wanted.

There was no getting around it. But how could she face her friends? How could she face Amira? Well . . . maybe her family could find another mosque to go to. Makayla made a mental note to look up more mosques tomorrow. She crawled into bed. It had been a long day, and she was far past ready for it to be over.

The next morning, her mother wasn't cooking breakfast, which was strange because she cooked breakfast every morning.

"No breakfast this morning," Makayla's mom said in answer to her puzzled look. "They're serving refreshments after the Eid prayer. Hurry and get dressed!"

Makayla was in no rush to go to the masjid, but she knew better than to make her mom late for anything. She quickly showered and made wudu. But she couldn't find her dress anywhere.

"Mom, where's my dress?" Makayla called from her room.

"Look in the back of your closet."

All Makayla saw in the back of her closet was her mom's garment bag.

"Why's your bag in my closet?" Makayla yelled.

"Just open it."

Makayla turned to see her mom standing in the doorway. She laid the bag across her bed and carefully unzipped it. It was her white dress inside, but it wasn't. Makayla ran her fingers along the purple embroidery and fluffed the layers of silver tulle her mom had added. With the creative fixes, it rivaled the fancy dress from the website. It was bigger, bolder, and more than Makayla thought she deserved.

"Eid Mubarak, Makayla." Mrs. Jackson held out a matching hijab that sparkled in the bedroom's light.

Teary-eyed, Makayla ran to give her mother a hug. "Happy Eid, Mom."

"What's with all the tears?" Mrs. Jackson chuckled.

"It's just so . . . and I acted so . . . and you did all this . . ." Makayla sobbed.

Mrs. Jackson wiped Makayla's eyes. "It's hard to see the beauty in things when you can't see past your insecurities."

"I'm sorry, Mom," Makayla said, barely above a whisper.

"Don't be sorry. Be confident." Mrs. Jackson picked her daughter's head up. "Now, let's hurry before we're late."

The Eid prayer was nothing like Makayla had imagined. It was prayer, but more fun. It was almost like a party. Everyone was in a good mood. There was tons of food. Everyone just seemed happy being together. Makayla stayed by her mother's side, happy to be sharing this new experience with her.

"There you are!" Amira grabbed Makayla by the shoulders and gave her three air-kisses. "You look great, but that's not the dress from the picture."

"You're right," said Makayla. "My mom made this for me." Makayla smiled at her mom and then proudly spun around in her dress.

"You look like a princess," said Amira. "Hey, Mrs. Jackson, think you could make me a dress next year?"

"Well, I usually only sew for family. But I guess I can consider it sadaqa."

"B-but I don't *need* charity." Amira's face turned red. "That doesn't make any sense."

"What can I say?" said Makayla. "Charity beats logic." Makayla doubled over laughing at her own joke.

"What does that even mean?" Amira shook her head and smiled. "You're so extra."

Mrs. Jackson and Amira talked fashion and the art of creative fixes while Makayla proudly showed her dress to the other girls. And that's how Makayla would always remember her first Eid—patched together, yet imperfectly perfect.

Taste

by Hanna Alkaf

When It happened, I lost my sense of
taste. I swear. I don't know how. But
it was as if each bud was switched off,
the way my abah switches off the lights in his store
at the end of the day—
one by one by one by one—
and with each flick of a switch, I lost another flavor:
Flick—sweet.
Flick—sour.
Flick—salty.
And on and on until nothing was left but a
darkness that weighed down my tongue and
made the food stick in my throat like
glue.

I didn't tell. Well, you can't, can you? Not
when you have a little brother to take care of and
your father's eyes grow squinty and worried, the lines
around the edges deepening when he stares at you
pushing food around your plate as if
that fools anybody.

You just can't talk about these things.
And especially not when you're twelve whole years old,
not when you're practically teenaged, which
is practically grown up, not even when
your father asks *How's your food?*

and you have to look him straight in the eye
as you say *Good*, not knowing anymore
whether it's
the food choking you
or the
lie.

Lontong is what we have on Eid morning every year,
   the men
returning from the mosque to steaming bowls
filled with kuah lodeh, the thick yellow gravy laden with
fresh vegetables and prawns, poured over
firm slices of nasi impit, rice packed tight, compacted
so it makes firm cakes that you can cut
into clean cubes or slices, then topped with lashings
   of fiery
sambal that stain the gravy a delicious, wicked red.
It's a tricky beast, lontong is. There are so many parts
   to it—
the rich and the creamy and the salty and sweet
   and spicy,
the crunch of deep-fried tempeh and the silky slipperi-
   ness of tofu,
and I have to make them all.
Somehow.

When It happened, Aiman began to have
waking nightmares, shrieking when
we had to get into the car
(and we always had to get into the car—
watching the Kuala Lumpur skyline spool past
in high-speed technicolor—
for school and sports and
for Quran reading classes and
to slowly sweat to death at the weddings
of people we didn't know but were apparently
related to somehow, and to buy groceries,
and most of all to see Mama, pale and white
in a narrow hospital bed, smiling but
there and not here with us),
kicking at the hands that held him,
no matter how loving, wailing as though his
car seat were a monster waiting to swallow him
    whole.
I won't I won't I won't I won't I WON'T,
so loud that his voice became scratchy
and Abah ducked his head, as if he could hide from
the prying eyes of our neighbors.

(No one can. I swear. They're equipped with sharp
gazes and sharper tongues, and nothing
cuts quite like the jabs that

fall from the lips of a
well-meaning Malay aunty.)

It's okay if you can't manage, Alia,
Abah had said that morning before he left for work,
smoothing damp hair back from my sweaty forehead.
We can buy some. Or we can do without. Either way,
we can make do. You know that, don't you?

But lontong *is* Eid.
And lontong is home,
and lontong is Mama,
even if Mama can't be here.
So lontong is what I'll make,
and lontong is what we'll have.

When It happened, my abah's eyes opened.
It was as if It had recentered his universe, as if
It shone bright spotlights on us:
AIMAN and ALIA, our names ringed
in colored lights above our heads,
reminding him that we exist.
He spends less time at the store, makes time
to pick us up from school, be home with us,

listens to our stories and eats with us at meals,
all of us carefully averting our eyes from the empty seat
    at the table,
and he says things Malay fathers don't always say,
    things like
Tell me what you think, and
Let's do it together, and
I love you.
And when he holds us, it's as if he's trying to
protect us from all the darkness in the world.

(The hugs are nice, but honestly,
nothing prepares you for the nightmares, or
the hole that's left when something that
was always there, constant, unwavering,
is suddenly no longer there.)

This isn't forever, the smiling lady in the white coat
    had said,
her lipstick creeping from her lips to her teeth in watery
    pink lines.
She'll be back before you know it; you probably
won't even have time to miss her!
And we'd laughed politely, as if it was funny, as if

this wasn't the silliest thing you could possibly say to
two children staring at the pale face of their mother, eyes
closed, skin leached of color by the harsh hospital lights,
hooked to machines that beeped like they did in
    the worst
medical dramas, where they yell *CODE BLUE* a lot and
there's blood everywhere and
there's always someone crying.
Always.

(I'm not supposed to watch those shows—
there's blood and violence
and *kissing* even, sometimes—
so don't tell my abah, okay?
Okay.)

Pity it had to happen just before Raya, though,
I'd heard her say to a blue-garbed nurse,
her voice quiet, her expression pitying.
Those poor kids.

And I'd burned with sudden rage.

I don't need your pity stares, fancy doctor lady,
or your fake concern, or the
jokes that fall flatter than my friend Rahel

that time she face-planted off her bicycle
trying to do wheelies in our driveway.

I'll take this Eid, and I'll make it good,
even if I have to do it myself,
even if the memory of It sometimes hits me
straight in the ribs and renders me breathless,
even if my tongue stays dark as midnight
without a moon.

I think about all of these things the night before Eid,
the blade of my knife slicing easily through firm white
tofu flesh,
wondering at the way It
darkened my tongue until it was numb
and loosened Aiman's until he could scream his fear
and softened Abah's until he could speak his love.

I wash and chop and slice and dice as the TV blares out
animated videos: baby sharks and hero pups,
holding Aiman captive under their spell,
and most of all I try to keep myself from thinking
about It.
Dried chilies, soaked in hot water so they part easily
under my blade,

yielding those stinging, biting seeds.

(*You have to get all of those out,* Mama had said, teasing out

the more stubborn ones carefully with the tip of her
knife.

Otherwise nobody will remember how the gravy tasted,
only how it burned their lips and their tongues.)

Shallots and garlic, quickly stripped of their skins.

Candlenuts, round and hard; lemongrass, but only the
white bits;

shrimp paste, toasted so that the smell fills the entire

house and makes Aiman cough (*Stop it, kakak!*).

An inch of the fresh turmeric and a handful of dried
shrimp—

no, that's too much, a little less than that.

Ginger and galangal, and woe betide you in

Mama's kitchen if you ever assumed they were

the same thing and tried to replace one with the other.

I run a finger over the knuckles of my right hand,
smiling at

the ghost of a hard rap from a wooden spoon

and Mama's voice, half laugh, half scold:

The taste is different, Alia!

As I'm grinding the spice paste, my
eyes watering from onion sweat, my nose

tingling from the sting of the chilies, Aiman wanders in, holding a stuffed puppy in his hands, all brown fur and bright pink clothes.

(*That's not a boy toy*, a big kid had sneered at him the
    other day
at the playground, with all the swagger that comes
    from two
extra years, three extra inches, and race-car-print pants.
That's a girl *toy. It's* pink, *and it's* fluffy.
And my tiny four-year-old brother had stared at
    him and
said simply: *It's a boy toy because it is mine, and I am*
    a boy.
And that was that.)

Kakak, he says, his voice plaintive but not quite a
    wail, not
yet. *Kakak, I'm hungry. What's for dinner?*
Each word lands on a jangled nerve, sending
sparks of irritation flowering through my chest.
What I want to do is say: *Go away and stop bothering me.*
What I want to do is say: *Can't you see I'm busy?*
What I want to do is snap.
Instead I think: *What would Mama say?*
And I take a deep breath
and glance at the clock, which is

ticking down the last couple of minutes to seven,
and I tell him: *Soon. Abah will be home soon.*
Can you wait awhile, sayang?

He frowns, bottom lip puffed way out.
Okay, he says finally over one shoulder as he leaves.
Fine. But only a tiny while.

(I used to call Aiman by his name, which means
    "fearless," or
adik, which means "little brother," or sometimes
monyet, which means "monkey,"
when he was in a monkeyish mood, climbing
everywhere, all sweat-soaked and
screeching with exuberance.

But sayang means "love," and it's what Mama calls us—
at least when we're not being monyets—
and even though it was weird at first, I like
hearing it around the house when she isn't
here, and I think Aiman does too.)

I'm still thinking about words as I pour oil carefully
    into a hot pan,
about the ways they twist and turn and dance, the
    way they

feel on my tongue, the way you can
mold them into new meanings, like the way you can
be sorry about something,
sorry for someone,
scoff at a sorry excuse, or
feel your heart soften at a sorry sight.
Or the way agak means "to guess" and
teragak-agak means "to hesitate," but
agak-agak, when cooking, means "to cook by feel,"
by instinct, to know in your bones each step that comes
    next.

Mama knew all about agak-agak.
(*Knows, Alia—Mama knows. Present tense.*)
Mama uses no recipes, curling her lip
ever so slightly if someone even so much as
suggests it, as if committing the steps to paper,
trapping them with words, erases their magic.
What do I need those for? she says, tapping her
    temple.
All my recipes are up here.
And it's true. Mama cooks as though the food
is part of her blood, leavening her bones:
A pinch of this, a dash of that, and
suddenly there it is, hot and steaming,
filling the whole house with warmth.

I toss slices of tofu and tempeh into the pan,
wincing at the tiny explosions that spatter hot oil onto
   my skin.
(*Don't!* Mama would say. *You must show it who's boss.*
The kitchen knows when you're afraid;
then the food tastes of nothing but your timidity.
Wield your tools with a firm grasp—your spatula,
your ladle, your knife. Stay in control.)
And as I watch them darken to golden brown, I wonder
how I can make a lontong that tastes as good as Mama's
when I can't taste anything at all.

Now for the main event: The gravy itself.
The one component that holds every
disparate thing together,
like mothers do in families.

I take a deep breath.
(*The kitchen knows when you're afraid.*)

Here we go.

Oil in the pot, just enough to coat the bottom;
when it begins to fizz, when the heat begins to rise
from the shimmering surface, in goes the spice paste,

hissing and spitting and yielding a host of familiar
   aromas,
making my stomach rumble and my eyes water.

Aiman wanders back in, puppy still clutched in his
   hands.
It smells like Mama in here, he remarks,
and I try very hard not to cry.
(Stay in control.)

Now I add water, creamy coconut milk, bay leaves.
   Bring the heat
down to a simmer, stir carefully, watch the gravy turn
   thick and golden.
Now I reach for the shelf where Mama keeps the
   tamarind paste,
the little glass jar faceted so it sparkles like a jewel in
   the light, topped
with a silver lid screwed on so tight I can't get it
   open.
Now I freeze, tears still in my eyes, smells still
dancing in the air, memories sticking in my throat
like the food I can't taste.

Now I remember.

Forever ago, or possibly just last week
(*Was it really just last week?*),
Mama had leaned close one morning,
a special twinkle in her eye, just for me.
This year, she'd said, quiet as though it was just for us
    to know,
this year you get to help me make the lontong.
And she'd handed me a long list and driven me to
    the store
and let me go in all by myself!
I remember the way my heart pounded
as I walked through the cramped aisles,
how I spent ages working out which ones
were candlenuts, too shy or too scared or too proud
to ask the boy at the checkout with the lurid manga
and the bored expression.

How carefully I pocketed the change, and how proud
    I felt
heaving the bags out to the car and seeing
my mother's smile, so warm it could have melted ice.
How crushed I felt seeing the ingredients laid out side
    by side
like sentinels on our kitchen counter, realizing I'd
    forgotten it:
tamarind paste for the juice Mama liked to add almost
    at the

very end, that hint of sour-sweetness deepening every other
flavor in the gravy, tying it all together
the way mothers do in families.

There were tears in my eyes then too, just the way
there were again later, when we found out, just the way
there are now.

Don't worry, sayang, Mama had said, her eyes soft,
    her voice
gentle as a caress. *I'll run back to the store and get some.*
She'd tweaked my nose. *It's not the end of the world, Alia.*
And she'd told me to be good and to mind Aiman as she
wound her hijab around her head and grabbed her
    car keys.

But it was the end of the world.
Because Mama never came back.
And it's all my fault.
All.
My.
Fault.

When Abah walks into the kitchen, red plastic bags
filled with sweating Styrofoam containers swinging
from his fingers, he finds me frozen in place, hands

still clutching a jar of tamarind paste, heaving as if
I may never be able to fill my lungs again, sobs
tearing at my throat like teeth.

I feel strong arms wrap around me and lift me up,
and when he holds me close it's as if he's trying
to protect me from all the darkness in the world.

And just what, he says finally, his voice a comforting
rumble against my cheek, *is going on here?*

(*I can't tell,* I think.
You just can't talk about these things, I think.)

But before I can stop myself the words spill out of
   me, skittering,
swarming, swooping in a confused stream, tripping over
themselves to escape from my chest.
My fault, I say, over and over and over.
My fault my fault my fault MY FAULT.

When I stop, there is silence, and I feel like
a piece of paper that's been crumpled, then
smoothed out again, all my lines and wrinkles
showing in the light. Abah rubs my back in comforting
little circles, letting the hiccups shudder through
my body before they die out altogether.

Seems to me like you've been carrying quite a load there, chickadee,
he says. *Why didn't you tell me sooner?*

Because Mama said, I tell him, sniffing.
Mama said to be good, and to mind Aiman,
and that's what I've been trying to do.

And you're very good at doing those things, he tells me.
But it's also okay to let other people take care of you.

We sit like that for a while, not talking, just kind of
being together, which is nice, the TV still blaring songs about
baby sharks and hero pups.

And maybe I should just stay that way, curled into my
father's chest.
Maybe I should just stay quiet and still, but
I know I can't.

Maaf zahir dan batin, I whisper, my voice little more
than the creak of a rusty door hinge.

Hmm?

Maaf zahir dan batin.
I make myself lean back, look him straight in the eye.
Mama told me it means that I'm sorry, that I'm sorry with
my whole body and heart and soul, and we always
say it during Eid because we're asking for forgiveness
for all our past wrongs so we can start fresh.
And I'm sorry; I'm so sorry. For the mess
I've made, for the whole sorry situation,
for everything.
Everything.

Abah sets me down on the floor and kneels, leaning close
so we're face-to-face, nose-to-nose.
It isn't your fault, chickadee, he says softly.
I know it feels like it is. But you can't control everything.
It isn't your fault that Mama decided to go to that store
instead of the one closer to home; it isn't your fault that
boy decided to cross the road right then; it isn't your fault that
the truck driver had to swerve to avoid him or that
he never saw Mama's car coming.
None of that is your fault; it isn't anyone's fault.
Sometimes things just happen, and we have to
accept them and move on. Even when it's hard.
Especially when it's hard.

And as he speaks, I feel the hard knot in my chest
slowly begin to unravel.

Now, Abah says, straightening up and surveying the
   mess,
what do we do about all this?

I rub my sleeve across my nose, leaving a trail of
   slimy snot.
You're *going to help me cook?* I ask.

His glance is withering. *Please. Your old man is a master
   at this.*
This ginger, for example . . .

That's galangal, Abah, I tell him, a giggle bubbling in
   my throat.

That's what I meant.

Together, with Aiman watching and calling out
his most helpful instructions, we pick up
where I left off. And while Abah assembles a
surprisingly passable sambal, I quietly open the jar
(and how odd, that what was so unyielding just minutes ago
suddenly gives its contents up to me so willingly)
and reach in, the tamarind paste soft and squishy to
   the touch.

How much do you need? Abah asks, his voice as gentle as the expression in his eyes.

Oh, you know, I say, shrugging. *Agak-agak.*

When the meal is ready, we sit around the table, our bowls
laden with firm slices of nasi impit and golden mounds of tofu
and tempeh, all swimming in rich gravy tinged a deep, warm
yellow, topped with dollops of bright red sambal like hats.
(*It's about time*, Aiman sniffs. *I'm* starving.)

We'll take some to Mama in the morning, Abah says.
Won't she be proud?
And then he asks the question
I've come to dread:
How's your food?

I take a breath. And I take a bite.
Good, I say. *Really good.*

And for the first time in days,
I'm not lying at all.

Eid Pictures

by Jamilah Thompkins-Bigelow

The Eid pictures on Ummi's phone—they glow,
delight and excite me, light up her screen like fireworks.
Flashy,
sparkly,
enchanting
pictures,
as I scroll along,
of Muslims celebrating,
taking and making joy—
a joy dazzling and dancing, loud and bold.

Pictures of hijabs and shaylas with patterns that never
    whisper,
of dashikis with colors that shout at my eyes,
bright garments making music as they glide against
    dark skin.
And lips painted loud, and teeth gleaming in smiles
    beaming proud,
city grills sizzling with flavor, smoking and popping,
city parks brimming with children, dashing and
    laughing,
too many people, too many prayer lines to fit on a
    phone screen,
too many to fit indoors.
I can almost hear the mighty cries of an imam with
    a mic.
Hundreds of voices say "ameen" as one.

The Eid pictures in my family's old photo albums,
   though—
they calm,
settle, and soothe me like Jedda's arms.
Soft,
cozy,
inviting
pictures
in plastic sleeves as I turn the pages,
of Muslims pioneering,
creating and establishing
warm traditions that hold me, loving and gentle.

Khimars swept back, satiny but simple,
and modest garments sewn during the quiet hush of
   the night,
heads covered by fezzes or kufis
and necks wrapped in dhikr beads or bow ties,
family-day fish-fries and the very first bean pies, creamy
   and sweet.
Pictures taken in a house or a temple or a mosque just built,
people bowing on carpet that smelled of incense and
   musk and home.
Small gatherings in the photos—small but strong.
I can almost hear Brother Imam reciting Quran like an
   old blues song.
A room of voices says "ameen" as one.

Picture Eid for the first Muslims who came to Ameri-
    can shores—came so long ago.
Close your eyes and picture them
in ships,
in chains,
enslaved.
Pictures
in their minds,
image after image of homes overseas,
of Muslims celebrating,
praying and living free
in the lands of Mansa Musa and the mosques of Sankoré.

Picture those Muslims in fields, looking out,
holding tight to memories of the past,
reaching out to visions of the future.
Did they foresee Eids bold and gentle?
Eids loud and loving?
Did they see their descendants—see you and me?
Did they see us all someday free?
I can almost hear their whispered wishes—
duas spoken in the fields each Eid.
Say "ameen" to those prayers,
all our voices as one.

Not Only
an Only

by Huda Al-Marashi

Aya had always liked her status as her school's only. Being the only Muslim and the only Iraqi made her the authority when anything came up in class remotely related to Islam, Arabs, or hummus.

Ever since one of the kids had brought a veggie tray with red pepper hummus to one of their classroom parties, Aya had been on a mission to make people understand that the word *hummus* means "garbanzo bean" in Arabic. Merely blending a bean or vegetable into a creamy paste did *not* magically transform it into the dish more accurately known as hummus bi tahina.

So when her class started their unit on Islam in social studies, Aya enjoyed her classmates' attention. During their first lesson, her peers wanted to know if she went to church, if she prayed five times a day like their textbook described, and if she fasted during Ramadan.

Aya shared that she did not go to church. She recited her five daily prayers at home because there wasn't a mosque or a masjid in town, and she fasted during the month of Ramadan, but not for the entire day yet because she was still too young.

But the next day, class felt different. Her teacher, Mrs. Johnson, had been calling on students to take turns reading through the chapter, and Aya couldn't help but notice that when Amanda Miller began reading aloud the paragraph on the difference between Sunnis and Shias, the rest of her classmates glanced at her as if they were studying her face for a reaction. Aya no longer felt like the classroom expert. Aya felt as if she were on display at a museum.

Aya tried to focus on following along in her textbook, but when the book described her sect, the Shias, as a radical group that broke away from mainstream Islam because they wanted the prophet Muhammad's successor to descend from the family line, Aya grew increasingly uneasy.

The word *radical* made it sound as if she belonged to the wrong side, but there was so much more to the story of her religion's division. Every year, Shias all over the world commemorated the martyrdom of the prophet Muhammad's grandson, and Aya knew it was that tragedy that had caused the eventual rift. However, she didn't feel like she remembered enough about those events to discuss them with her class.

Aya wanted to at least try and raise an objection to this summary, but before she had the chance, Amanda looked over at her and asked, "Which sect are you?"

Aya's heart sank.

"I'm a Shia, but we're not radicals," Aya said, feeling immediately dissatisfied with her answer. She searched her mind for something more convincing to add, but this time Amanda's closest friend, Samantha, chimed in to ask if Aya celebrated Christmas.

Aya held in a sigh. Amanda's family hosted a huge

Christmas party every year, and they invited Amanda's entire group of friends and their families. For weeks leading up to the event, Amanda regaled the class with every detail of her family's decorations and plans. There was the huge tree that scraped the ceiling; the white lights that trimmed her house; the wreaths that were tied to every window; and the cookie exchange that allowed every guest to go home with a tin full of assorted treats. Even though Aya couldn't imagine her parents at Amanda Miller's party, she couldn't help but feel that how she answered this question would somehow forfeit her chance of ever being invited.

"We don't really celebrate Christmas," Aya said. "But we have two major Eids every year, so it's kind of like having Christmas twice."

Amanda made a doubtful expression and exchanged a look with Samantha before asking, "How is it like Christmas? Do you decorate and get presents?"

This was a sore spot for Aya. She knew that whatever celebrations her family had, they did not rival Amanda's family's elaborate Christmas. Aya's parents rarely took the day off for Eid, and her family didn't really belong to a Muslim community anymore. Their small agricultural town only had a handful of other Muslims. They all used to take turns praying in each other's houses, but a few years ago, when it was Aya's parents' turn to host the weekly prayers, her father had overheard someone remark that Shias weren't real Muslims. Her parents had taken this as a hint that they weren't welcome, and they'd stopped going, too uncomfortable to tell anyone why.

It hadn't taken long for Aya to get used to praying at home with her family. None of the Muslim families in town had children her age, so there was no one in particular whom she missed. Except on Eid. Then it was hard to have nowhere special to go, nothing to do.

Aya thought of the Eid coming up next month and how it would likely be no different. Aya would pray with her parents and grandparents at home and then arrive at school an hour late, like she'd been at a doctor's appointment. But Aya couldn't bear to share such boring plans with Amanda.

"We do get presents, and we wear all new clothes and go to a prayer in the morning. And then after that there's usually a carnival with food and games."

Aya didn't mention that she'd never actually been to an Eid carnival, that she'd only heard about them from her cousins who lived in larger cities and had told her about their masjids' huge celebrations. That was another benefit of being an only that Aya hadn't given much thought to until now—she didn't have to worry about anyone else in school contradicting her.

Aya quickly glanced over at Amanda to see if she'd convinced her, and she was relieved to see Amanda shrug in Samantha's direction, as if she was satisfied by Aya's answer. Aya released the sigh she'd been holding and hoped that one day her family's Eid would be as fun as the Eid she'd described.

A few weeks later, Aya's mother sent her to school with a note to tell Mrs. Johnson that she'd be missing the following Monday morning for Eid. Aya begged her mother to excuse her for the whole day so Amanda would think she'd been at a carnival, but Aya's mother insisted that she had to work and there was no sense in her staying home.

Aya walked into the classroom with her head down, her gaze fixed on the note in her hand. When she looked up, she was surprised to see a new girl standing beside Mrs. Johnson's desk. A new girl with an off-white, no-fuss, one-piece hijab slipped over her head.

Aya's mouth dropped open, and she instinctively reached up and smoothed her uncovered hair. She didn't know anyone who wore hijab in sixth grade. She reached for her gold necklace with the pendant that said "Allah" in Arabic script. That was the only thing Aya wore that gave her away as Muslim.

"Oh, good, Aya. I'm glad you're here," Mrs. Johnson said. "This is Hana. She just moved here from the Bay Area. I thought you could show Hana around since you're both Muslim."

Aya felt a hot prickle of frustration that Mrs. Johnson assumed she'd want to be friends with Hana because of their shared religion, but when she looked over at Hana, she saw that Hana wore a knowing expression. She'd picked up on the awkwardness too.

Aya offered a weak shrug, as if she were apologizing for Mrs. Johnson, and in return, Hana waved and said, "Assalamu Alaikum."

Aya was taken aback. She had never used this greeting with a peer, only with her parents and grandparents, aunts and uncles, and here was Hana, uttering a Muslim hello as if she'd said it to friends many times before.

Aya nervously spun the two slender gold bangles on her wrist and replied, "Walaikumussalaam."

At Mrs. Johnson's request, Aya showed Hana to her desk, then walked back to her own, trying to find a name for her mixed feelings. Hana seemed friendly and kind, but she also seemed more Muslim than Aya was. Hana probably *did* go to Eid carnivals and had been going her entire life. What if she became the classroom's new expert? Or worse, what if she was the type of Sunni who thought Aya wasn't a real Muslim too?

Aya shook her head to rid herself of the ridiculous thought. She heard her mother's voice, reminding her that they were all Muslims first. And it might be nice to no longer be the classroom only. But the uneasy knot in her stomach lingered, and Aya was distracted all through morning math, wondering what she was going to do with Hana at lunch. Should she go off and sit where she always sat, on the picnic table under the tree, with the girls who spent recess drawing, crocheting, and weaving friendship bracelets? Should she invite Hana to join her or leave her to find her own group of friends? Maybe Hana hated crafts and Aya should reassure her that they didn't have to be friends just because they were both Muslim?

At the sound of the bell, Aya grabbed her lunch from her backpack, but before she could head out the classroom door, Hana was at her side with her lunch box in hand. "So where do you usually have lunch?" she asked.

Again, Aya felt a bristle of annoyance. Hana was so confident and comfortable that Aya was starting to feel like *she* was the new girl. Aya made the split-second decision not to introduce Hana to her friends over at the craft table and pointed Hana to the unoccupied table at the edge of the playground.

For a moment, the two girls sat facing each other without much to say. They set up their lunches, pulling out their containers and peeling off their lids, and then almost simultaneously their gazes fell on each other's food. They both had rice, left over from yesterday's dinner.

Hana was the first to say, "Do you ever wish you could just have a sandwich?"

Aya laughed. Hard. Harder than she'd ever laughed at school. "Every single day."

Hana laughed too, and added, "My grandma packs me so much food—way more than I could ever eat at lunch—and I'm always like, 'Can't I just have peanut butter and jelly?'"

"Do you live with your grandma?" Aya asked.

"I don't just *live* with my grandma, I share a room with her. And I love her biryani, but not cold. And not at school."

Aya giggled. "I share a room too! And not even with a sister. I share a room with my brother!" Aya told Hana how her grandparents had moved in with her family and how they had taken over her brother's room, so he had to bunk with her. Hana shared that her family was from Pakistan and that she loved pizza nights because then she could bring those leftovers to school. Aya added that her family was from Iraq and that they also had a rice dish called biryani even though it had different ingredients and flavors.

Aya couldn't get over how much she had in common with Hana, and she grew so involved in their conversation that she didn't notice when Amanda and her band of friends approached their table.

"What are you guys eating?" Amanda asked.

It was an innocent question, but Aya felt a burst of concern. She tried to keep the conversation about food for as long as possible, nervous that Amanda would bring up something more sensitive, like her sect. She was just getting to know Hana, and she didn't want Amanda steering their conversation toward their differences before they'd had a chance to discuss them on their own.

But Amanda had already moved on to Hana's hijab. "Why do you wear that if Aya doesn't?"

"Because I choose to," Hana said.

"Doesn't it make you hot?"

"Only if it's hot out."

"Do you wear it when you go swimming?"

"No. I have a different hijab for swimming."

"How about in the shower?"

"No."

"And when you're sleeping?"

"No."

Aya marveled at Hana's tone. It was patient but firm, and by not offering up detailed explanations and answers, she was showing Amanda without having to say it that she did not care to carry on the conversation.

Amanda, however, did not pick up on Hana's disinterest, and she asked the question Aya had been dreading: "What are you, a Sunni or a Shia?"

Hana gave Amanda and her friends a puzzled look. "What do you even know about Sunnis and Shias?"

Aya hung her head in embarrassment. Amanda didn't know that this was an awkward question for them both. Most Muslims avoided bringing attention to their differences, and although people eventually figured out each other's sects, they rarely asked this question, especially not within moments of meeting one another.

Amanda said, "We read in class that Aya is a radical, but she says she's not."

Aya was too stunned to react. She searched for words, but before she could say anything, Hana said, "Because she's not. We're all Muslims, and that's all that matters."

Aya felt a mix of relief and confusion. *She* was supposed to be the classroom only, but having Hana speak up for her was comforting in a way Aya had never known before.

Amanda rolled her eyes, and Hana gave Aya a look of exasperation that Aya found great satisfaction in returning.

Amanda finally got the hint that the conversation had ended. She motioned to her friends that it was time to walk away, and as Aya watched Amanda retreat, she was surprised by the rush of warmth she felt for Hana. It was a feeling she hadn't thought was possible when she'd seen her standing at Mrs. Johnson's side only a few hours ago.

"Tough crowd," Hana said, and the girls found themselves giggling again.

"But seriously," Hana added, "you must be the only Muslim they've ever met. In my old school there were at least thirty Muslim kids, and some were Shia, so don't worry. I know you're not a radical. I don't know how you've survived alone all this time. Alhamdulillah, we have each other, right?"

"Yeah," Aya said. "It's pretty great."

"And at least we'll have each other at prayers. I hear the community here is super small and people pray at each other's homes. Are you guys sticking around town for Eid?"

Aya's shoulders slumped. After Amanda's interrogation, she didn't want to bring up their differences again and tell Hana that her family no longer felt welcome in the community. "We actually prefer to pray at home," she said instead. "My grandfather leads us."

"But that's no fun," Hana said. "You guys have to start coming now that I'm here so we can hang out."

Aya's breath quickened. "I don't think that's going to happen, Hana. It's just that someone said some things about Shias not being real Muslims, and now my parents don't like to go."

Hana's eyes widened with shock. "That's so messed up, Aya! That would never happen at our masjid where I used to live. It's a totally mixed community—and not just Sunni and Shia mixed, but cultures and languages too. You have to come with us. We're driving back up for Eid. It's just over an hour from here, and so many people come that they actually have to rent out the convention center! And after the prayer, there's a carnival, and food, and vendors selling all kinds of stuff like scarves and prayer mats and tasbih. And I finally get to wear my new shalwar kameez and all my bangles. Something tells me you're a bangle kind of girl too."

Aya looked down at her bangles. She never took them off. She loved their soft jingle as she went about her day, and going to a *carnival* sounded equally lovely. She could have the kind of Eid she'd described to Amanda and come back to school with her own stories to tell of friends, food, and fun. She didn't know if her parents would agree to go, but she was already enchanted by the idea. How amazing would it be to actually feel like it was Eid?

"It's for everyone," Aya told her mother as they cleared off the dinner table that night. "My new friend Hana said all Muslims are welcome. And she said that everyone gets dressed up and that she's going to wear a new shalwar kameez and bangles up to her elbows. I wish we were Pakistani like Hana's family. How come Arabi people never wear their cultural clothing? We dress the same to everything."

Aya's mother looked at her with a puzzled expression, a stack of dirty plates in her hands. "You don't have to be Pakistani to dress up. You can wear the gelabeya your aunty sent you."

Aya had completely forgotten about the turquoise full-length gown hanging in the back of her closet. It had a beautiful sheer overlay with a trim of silver beads along the neckline and down its bodice. She'd never had an occasion to wear it before.

"Wait," Aya said, pointing at her mother with a handful of dirty forks and spoons. "Does that mean we can go?"

"I don't know, habibti. The convention center is far, and both your father and I had planned to go to work. But we'll see. Insha'Allah."

God willing.

Aya couldn't believe it. Her mother was actually considering it. Their local Eid had always been such a quiet affair with so few families, but now she might have the chance to plan an Eid outfit to wear to Eid prayers with a friend. That night, Aya breezed through loading the dishwasher, feeling something she'd never felt about Eid before—excitement.

Eid morning, Aya's family woke up for their dawn prayers, and instead of rushing to pray and heading off to work, Aya's parents surprised her with the news that they'd made plans to join Hana's family at the convention center.

Aya couldn't believe that her parents had agreed to go. She rattled off a string of thank-yous and hurried to her bedroom, where she slid on her gelabeya. Then she stood in front of her dresser mirror, wrapping her hair in a scarf that matched the trim on her dress. She liked the way the hijab framed her face, and it made her think about Hana, how they'd match.

Aya's family piled into their minivan, her parents in the front row, grandparents in the middle, and kids in the back. After more than an hour of driving through large stretches of farmland, tall buildings appeared on the horizon. Aya's mother maneuvered the van through a maze of traffic before they finally pulled into a multilevel parking structure. Aya studied the people leaving their cars, the women in scarves and the men in skullcaps and their clothes that came in every shade of the rainbow. Aya's family joined the stream of people headed inside the main building. In the hallways, they passed food stalls and pop-up shops selling scarves, books, games, puzzles, incense, candles, and prayer mats. Aya had never seen so many Muslims in one place, and she didn't know how she'd possibly find Hana in this crowd.

But Hana was right at the main door, waiting for her with a group of girls their age. "Eid Mubarak, Aya," Hana said, and wrapped Aya in a hug. She turned to her friends and added, "You guys, this is my savior, the one I told you about," and then she handed Aya a small paper-wrapped package.

Inside, Aya found a stack of turquoise glass bangles, the same shade as her gelabeya.

"I know you have your gold bangles, but now you can match the rest of us," Hana said.

Aya slid her new accessories onto her wrist, feeling as if she'd been given a treasure. This was the first Eid gift she'd ever gotten from a friend. Aya thought back on all the Eids that had passed in a blurred rush—her family saying their Eid prayers together in the morning, her parents rushing off to work after taking Aya and her siblings to school—and she felt a joy she'd never known before on this special holiday.

Aya glanced at Hana and saw her gesturing for Aya to hurry and join everyone for the prayer. She ran toward Hana and her friends, delighting in the delicate clinking sound of her new bangles. Aya stood shoulder to shoulder with Hana, her breath catching with sheer delight at the row after row of people lined up to pray.

At one point in the prayer, most of the congregation folded their hands and rested them across their stomachs, as was Sunni custom. Aya left her hands at her sides and caught sight of several other people in the room doing the same. Hana was right. This was a mixed community, and it truly did not matter whose hands were folded and whose hands were straight when everyone's lips moved in sync, reciting the words to the same prayers; when everyone bowed at the exact same moment; and when everyone's hearts were so warm.

Hana and Aya moved into sujood, pressing their foreheads to the floor, and Aya wondered why she had ever wanted to be her classroom's only. It was so much better being an only together.

Maya Madinah Chooses Joy

by Ayesha Mattu

Maya Madinah Mu'min could not bear this joy for one more second. She fled to her room to escape the laughter and singing that was filling her candy-colored Victorian house. Even from there, she could hear her family and friends celebrating the bittersweet end of Ramadan at the Mu'mins' annual Chand Raat party. Their togetherness left her tight and breathless with loneliness and anxiety. She wanted to crawl out of her skin. She had to get away.

No, not just get away. Run away. Without any clear plan beyond getting away from the house and the corresponding constriction in her heart, she threw a few essentials into her sturdy red backpack: The worn copy of *Travel Light* that she and Daddy had read together every night Before Everything Changed; Butch, the stuffed Rottweiler; and her latest snack obsession, itsy-bitsy violet champagne grapes.

She crept out her open window, dropping onto all fours to crawl under the other windows that were spilling light, warmth, and the fragrance of cardamom into the mist-laced air, and made her way to the front of the house. Scuffing her brown toes in the succulent garden, Maya Madinah glanced down. Great. No shoes. How far could she run without shoes? She grabbed her gardening flip-flops from the front porch, where they were sitting near the neat rows of guest shoes, turned around, and ran straight into Billa.

"I can't stand it anymore!" she scowl-whispered to the fat marmalade neighborhood cat. Billa paused in his ambling, then settled down close enough to listen—though he closed his eyes so as not to appear too eager.

Maya Madinah rolled her own eyes heavenward, where the Shawwal crescent moon had hung before the San Francisco fog had swept in to obscure it. She glanced over at Billa again. Well, a half-cocked feline ear was better than none.

Maya Madinah put down her flip-flops and stroked the enormous cat as they sat together on the porch steps. Billa was a comforting, purring solidity in her shifting world. Hot tears began leaking out of her eyes at the thought of the changes over the past year. She still lived in the same house with Mama, but everything else was different. Worse. Daddy had moved out last year. The divorce had been finalized last month.

She thought back to the last Eid-ul-Fitr they had shared as a real family, almost a year ago now. How they had craned their necks outside to look for the crescent moon that heralded the entwined beginnings and endings of Islamic months. How they had welcomed their community in for the Chand Raat party that began their Eid celebrations. The mehndi and songs from Mama's Pakistani ancestors; the bright paper lanterns and enthralling stories from Daddy's people—Black Muslims, as American as bean pie. Faith, feasting, and family: all of the things that made Ramadan—and life—sweet.

At the beginning of Ramadan every year, Daddy dusted off the wooden calendar he had made for her in his garage workshop when she was three. The calendar still sported a few faded Thomas the Tank Engine stickers. She had so loved those books. Each little door on the calendar was decorated with a hand-painted picture of the corresponding moon phase for that evening, marking the start of a new day of fasting. Daddy placed a dark chocolate—her favorite and his—inside each nook, one chocolate for every day of the month and a small toy for every sacred Friday.

"Begin each day with sweetness and remembrance," he reminded her with that gentle, lingering caress on her head that always felt like a blessing. At the end of the month, there were more gifts for Eid, but that calendar was special. Daddy had made it just for her. Even when he spent long days at work or had to travel during Ramadan, he never forgot to fill it. Though she had seen him every weekend since he'd moved out, her home and heart still felt empty without his daily presence.

This year, Mama had forgotten to put the calendar up at first. When she finally remembered, she had stocked one nook with colorful candies instead of dark chocolate—and another with cashews! Even now, the audacity made Maya Madinah stomp her feet, startling Billa.

"Sorry for scaring you, Billa. I like moon nuts, but they don't belong in the Ramadan calendar! I got really mad after that. You probably heard me screaming at my mom." Maya Madinah's voice trailed off as she remembered how she had yelled, "I hate you!" before storming off to her room.

Maya Madinah had never seen her mother cry until that day. Just thinking about it now made the knot of fear and anxiety she'd carried in her stomach since Daddy left grow larger. She wondered if anything would ever be the same again.

Blinking away renewed pinpricks of tears, Maya Madinah slipped her feet into her flip-flops and glanced at Billa, who now appeared to be pretending to sleep.

"Useless cat," she muttered fondly, prodding him with her finger.

He purred in response, stretching out for more.

"Where should I go, Billa?" she asked, stroking his fat belly. "Daddy is in Oakland, and I've never ridden that far on BART alone." She glanced down at the kids' Clipper Card for public transit that she'd had since she was five years old, hanging, as always, from her backpack.

Billa stretched and meowed, waving a languid paw toward the sloping hillside. *Nusaybah!* Maya Madinah's smile lit up her face—her khala lived a few blocks away.

"Of course! Nusaybah Khala will know what to do. Billa, you're brilliant. Grumpy, but brilliant."

Maya Madinah opened the front gate, grateful that the noise inside the house would drown out its squealing hinges. She set off on the familiar unpaved path known only to neighborhood residents that linked her street to others nearby and eventually led to Glen Canyon. Solar lights dotted the path, lighting her way through wild fennel and poppies.

Maya Madinah's heart was beating fast with excitement as she rushed uphill. She thought about Mama again. They had often walked together on this very path. They loved watching the city from the hilltop as the sun set, pointing out the blue water tower and other familiar landmarks before they were swallowed by the billowing fog. Mama had shared tales of women from the city, such as Ina Coolbrith, the first poet laureate of any state, and Maya Angelou—her namesake!—the first Black San Francisco streetcar conductor, novelist, and so, so much more.

"This, too, is your heritage," Mama had whispered, holding her close, and Maya Madinah had felt the glow in her stomach of roots and belonging and pride. But now her stomach tightened again. It had been a long time since they'd had a conversation like that.

At the crest of the hill, Maya Madinah paused, panting a little, the fog gently crowning her tight, dark curls with tiny, wet stars. She opened the gate latch and slipped past the first larger house to peek at the tiny, lit cottage tucked in the yard behind it.

Nusaybah Khala was home tonight.

Relieved, Maya Madinah knocked gently on the door, and an instant later, she was taking off her shoes and stepping into a warm hug that made her want to cry and laugh at once, instantly filled with love for her adored Nusaybah Khala.

"Habibti! Did you come to get me for the party? I'm sorry I'm late. Planning the Hikayatna workshop has been taking up all my time," Nusaybah said, pushing back her blue-streaked hair. She was referring, Maya Madinah knew, to the preservation of post-Nakba Palestinian diaspora stories.

Maya Madinah paused before answering, unsure now if her aunt would understand her need to escape. "Is that a new painting?" she stalled, wandering over to the large abstract canvas in the corner. Nusaybah's cottage was one of Maya Madinah's favorite places. Filled with paintings and books, it looked like the sort of place that she'd like to live in that faraway time called Grown Up.

"Yes, love. Often, after the workshops, my mind swirls with colors connected to the stories I've heard. I have to paint to release them," Nusaybah answered.

Maya Madinah turned to face her aunt. "I'm not here to take you to the party," she admitted. Now the words spilled out fast. "I'm running away—and I need your help! I don't know where to go. Maybe I could stay with you? Or maybe you could help me get to Daddy's apartment? I've never taken the train alone at night."

Maya Madinah crossed her arms, lower lip pouting a little in unconscious defiance, legs spread firm and wide to underline her immovable resolve.

Instead of the shocked reaction Maya Madinah expected, Nusaybah's hazel eyes continued gazing into hers, as unruffled as Billa's, as if young girls marched into her studio every day, announcing plans to run away.

"Well then, you'll need some shay to warm you up before your journey," Nusaybah said in an unperturbed voice, turning on the quick electric kettle in her studio and rummaging around for black tea, sugar, and herbs.

Maya Madinah blinked in surprise, arms dropping to her sides. She found she could breathe a little more deeply now.

Maya Madinah loved her aunt's ease with silence and her deep listening. So many adults she knew only pretended to listen when in fact they were just waiting for her to pause so they could jump in and lecture her. She browsed her aunt's bookshelves in the comfortable silence, glancing over occasionally as her aunt made Palestinian-style tea. Mama sometimes let Maya Madinah have sips of her morning chai, slow-simmered with PG Tips tea and whole milk in the Punjabi way. Daddy preferred black coffee, taking the time to hand-grind the beans for the French press. Maya Madinah loved the smell of coffee but not yet the taste, though she kept trying. She missed the smell of coffee in the house.

Her aunt handed her a cup of tea. It was sweet, with chamomile flowers floating on the surface. She noticed that the cup was one of her aunt's special ones that she kept up on the top shelf for sharing tea with other adults. But then, Maya Madinah supposed she must be Grown Up now that she had left home.

The thought gave her a shiver of anxiety—and excitement.

"Now tell me everything," Nusaybah said as they sat close together at the tiny, half-moon-shaped dining table for two against the wall.

"Everyone at the Chand Raat party was so happy that it made me mad. Even Mama was smiling and laughing. How can she be so happy after everything that's happened? It's like she doesn't care how I feel! Nobody does!" Maya Madinah felt the anxiety unspool and soften a little more in her core. Tears rushed out.

Her aunt murmured sounds of love and moved her chair closer so she could put her arm around Maya Madinah's shoulders, still listening.

"Nothing is the same since Daddy moved out. It didn't feel like a proper Ramadan, and now it doesn't feel like a real Eid! Mama didn't even ask me if she could invite all those people over for Chand Raat. She might be happy, but I'm not. And I never will be until we are a real family again," Maya Madinah said, words broken between sobs.

Her belly felt softer now from sharing some of the emotions that had filled her for the past year and that she had been unable to tell anyone about until tonight. Not the kind therapist her parents had found for her or the school counselor who occasionally checked in. Not even her parents, who had assured her that she could talk to them but who were each now in their separate homes.

How could she tell her parents her deepest prayer that somehow they could be a family again?

"I'm so glad you shared that with me, habibti. You have been carrying so much so bravely for such a long time." Nusaybah Khala stroked Maya Madinah's curls, her love and empathy palpable between them. "Would it be okay if you spent the night here before deciding what you want to do next?"

Maya Madinah nodded, wiping her tear-streaked face. Staying with Nusaybah Khala was always a special treat. She was beginning to miss Mama a little but was not yet ready to go home. She wondered if her mother had even noticed she was gone. She hoped so, and she hoped Mama was worried. *Serves her right!*

"May I let your mother and father know we have decided to have a Chand Raat slumber party here tonight?" Nusaybah asked.

"I suppose so." Maya Madinah shrugged after a minute of thought. "They'll probably be angry and say no, though."

"No one will be angry with you, darling. I just don't want them to worry," Nusaybah said before typing a text and putting away her phone. "Why don't we get ready for bed first? Then we can talk some more and have a bedtime story, if you like?"

Maya Madinah nodded. Her khala always had the best stories. She took the too-large flannel pajamas her aunt offered her into the bathroom, rolling up the soft sleeves and hems to make them fit.

Nusaybah rolled out the trundle bed from underneath her bed frame and tucked Maya Madinah in with Butch, her stuffed dog. Butch was a love-worn gift from her father, and without him she could not sleep. All night she kept her arms wrapped tightly around him, as if he were a buoy keeping her afloat in her dreams.

"You've heard this story before, though perhaps not in this way. Because now you are someone new, revisiting an old story and mining it for more," Nusaybah said.

"How am I new, Nusaybah Khala?" Maya Madinah asked.

"We are made anew every day, beloved. And tasting sadness changes us," Nusaybah said. "Like so many of the best stories, this one begins in a faraway land, long ago. There was a little boy swimming inside his mother, waiting to be born. But shortly before the day of his birth, his father passed away. He was raised by his tender, grief-stricken mother and a wet nurse, who loved him like he was her own son. For a while, his world was solid and stable, but when his mother also passed away, he was still only five years old!

"Next he went to live with his grandfather until the loving old man passed away when the boy was eight. After that, the boy lived with a dear uncle until he was a young man, ready to make his way in the world." Nusaybah paused. "Of course, you know who this is, don't you?"

Maya Madinah nodded. She had heard the story of his childhood many times, though this was the first time she had felt his sadness and loss so keenly in her own heart. "The Prophet Muhammad, peace be upon him."

"That's right! He was heartbroken so many times, and yet he continued to try to be brave enough to love and be loved again. Joy and sorrow follow each other endlessly like moon phases, Maya Madinah. There are times of shining fullness and times of emptying out. Sometimes, before we can welcome joy in again, we need to acknowledge the sadness in our hearts—as you did so courageously tonight, my love," Nusaybah said, squeezing her tight.

"What you are going through is painful. I am grateful that both of your parents are still here to walk beside you, but it is still hard." She paused again before asking, "When it was the Prophet's turn to form a family, what do you think it looked like?"

Maya Madinah considered. This was the first time she had been asked to reflect on his life in such a personal way. From all the stories she'd heard growing up, it seemed like he had been surrounded by many loving people for most of his life. Kind of like she had been, growing up in this little village within the city.

"Big, fun, and busy?" Maya Madinah ventured. "He had family, best friends, and a village full of people of different races, classes, and faiths. He lived close to the people he loved, and his home was always open to them. They helped him when things got hard. And he loved cats!"

"Yes, that's certainly all true!" Nusaybah laughed. "He lived with partners and children—both biological and adopted—and had deep friendships and a strong community. You know, he was given many difficulties in his life, but he chose to build on those experiences by creating a world of beauty, love, joy, and connection for himself and those around him."

Maya Madinah thought about it. Before Everything Changed, that's what her world had been like too.

"But I want my mom and dad around. I know life can be hard, but I need them both. Together," Maya Madinah said.

"I know, sweetheart. It's totally natural and okay for you to feel that way," Nusaybah assured her. "Families can look a lot of different ways, Maya Madinah. And each of them is beautiful. We each have a biological family, the one we're born into. You have your parents and relatives. And we each have a chosen family, which might include people we are related to *and* those we aren't. Look at us! We may not be related by blood, but I am so glad to have you as my chosen niece."

Here, Nusaybah bent over Maya Madinah's drowsing head. "Sleep and dream and grow now, beloved. When you wake up, you will know where to go from here. Listen to the One in your deepest heart and then trust yourself. Good night."

Maya Madinah closed her eyes, hugging Butch tight, her one sharp desire throbbing as a prayer in her heart before sleep overcame her.

Early-morning sunlight streamed through the sheer white curtains, nudging Maya Madinah awake. She was

alone in the cottage but unafraid. Nusaybah had probably popped into her parents' home a few feet away.

It was Eid.

Her first Eid without her family, she realized, her
stomach clenching with that familiar knot again. She
put her hands over her belly, breathing deeply to loosen
the tightness. "It's okay to feel this way," she murmured
aloud, voice quavering.

She missed her mother and father with a fierceness
now, remembering how Mama always kissed her gently on the forehead to wake her for Eid prayers at the
mosque and how her father held her little hand gently in
his big brown one as they prayed together, side by side.

Well, Maya Madinah thought, reflecting on the conversation from last night, it was her first Eid without her
family *as they had been* for a long time. If they couldn't be
what they had been, *could* they become something new?
She wasn't sure. But maybe it was worth trying—one
breath, one day at a time. She lay staring up through the
skylight at the radiant blue sky, hands behind her head,
thinking some more.

"It's going to be hard. It's going to be different. But
I can try," she said finally, turning to Butch, feeling both
courage and sadness rise in her heart.

After the cathartic cry and conversation and a good
night's sleep, she felt lighter and stronger and almost—but
not quite—ready for this strange new Eid ahead. If it

included tears and laughter, that was okay, because she would be with—what had her khala called it?—her chosen family. All those whom she loved, who loved her in return, including Butch and Billa and her favorite books.

She thought about the Eid plans her parents had discussed with her a few days ago. At the time, she had felt rebellious and angry. All she had wanted then was for them to spend the whole day together. Now, for the first time, she felt a trace of curiosity. Maybe having two separate Eid outings wouldn't be as bad as she had thought.

She was going to spend the morning with Mama and her maternal cousins and friends at the huge Eid festival at the Santa Clara County Fairgrounds with cotton candy and rides. Then Daddy was going to pick her up and take her to the Unity Eid picnic in Oakland, and she would see Imam Al Amin from her favorite mosque, feast on delicious barbecue while listening to a band, and play with her paternal cousins and still more friends.

In each place, she would be surrounded by family and friends. Her chosen family. Big. And fun. And busy. She would be just like Muhammad.

Maya Madinah grinned and sat up, her glorious curls reaching heavenward.

Suddenly, she couldn't wait for this new and different Eid to begin.

Eid and Pink Bubble Gum, Insha'Allah

by Randa Abdel-Fattah

I f you touch your tongue while yawning, it can stop the yawn. It's a scientific fact."

I closed my eyes and took a deep breath, trying to distract my mind as my brother Noor's voice droned on.

"Do you know that *anatidaephobia* is the fear that somewhere in the world, there is a duck watching you? I mean, how wild would it be to have that phobia?!"

I snapped. "You know what's wild?! Having to listen to you recite stupid trivia on an eight-hour road trip! Quit it!"

"Kids, stop fighting," Mum called out in a bored tone.

Noor was unperturbed. "It's not a stupid fact. Somewhere out there in the galaxy there are probably aliens sharing random stupid facts about us human beings. Sheez."

I stared at him, open-mouthed. He stared back at me and flashed a cheesy smile.

"What?" he asked innocently.

I didn't have a chance to respond, because Adam (four years old, going on three) and Hannah (five years old, going on four) were in the middle row of seats, fighting over a book that neither had been interested in until one of them had touched it, setting off a sudden property war. Dad was driving, trying to listen to his CD (a religious lecture on how to control your temper when fasting), and Noor's nose was back in his *1,001 Random Facts* book.

"Do you hear what the sheikh is saying, children?" Dad said. "We have to avoid anger when we're fast—"

"Adam and Hannah, will you learn to share!" Mum yelled angrily, turning around to glare at them as she reached over and grabbed the book. The spine ripped, provoking hysterical wails from them both.

"Easy for this sheikh to say," I muttered. "He's never been on a road trip with these brats."

Mum shoved lollipops into Hannah's and Adam's hands, which shut them up instantly. Then she calmly turned off the stereo. Dad didn't dare protest.

I looked longingly at the lollipops and then glanced at my watch: three hours until we broke the last fast in the month of Ramadan. I threw my head back against the seat and sighed.

"Did you know a cockroach can live for up to one week without its head?"

"The more important question," I couldn't help but snap back, "is how much longer you're going to live if you continue with the trivia."

We were on a road trip. It was our annual Eid-ul-Fitr ritual: driving to visit my grandparents, who lived on the south coast outside of Sydney, to spend the holiday with them.

Once upon a time, I was the only child in the family. The first-born daughter who had her parents' full attention and adoration. Road trips were simple then. My parents smiling lovingly at me, giving in to my every demand. No sharing toys or gadgets, crusts delicately cut off my sandwiches, no question of who chose the entertainment. It was just me. Life was great. Then when I was four, a brother, Noor, arrived. It took some time to adjust, but the ratio was at least equal: one child per parent. Then a few years later, another girl unexpectedly arrived: Hannah. And then another boy, Adam. My parents clearly had no mathematical comprehension. Didn't they realize they were outnumbered? Nobody felt it more acutely than me. I'd gone from 100 percent attention to 25 percent—on a good day! And as if that weren't bad enough, I barely had time to myself because I was the eldest, and with my parents outnumbered, they relied on me a lot: *Can you make sure Hannah doesn't climb the fridge while I take a shower? Can you take them on the trampoline while I mow the lawn? Can you make sure Adam doesn't play soccer with the eggs while I send this e-mail?*

We were due to arrive at my grandparents' place late at night. We had taken off four hours before sunset; Noor, Mum, Dad, and I had decided we could cope with the fast while traveling. It was only for a few hours.

But we were fasting while feeding Adam and Hannah, using food as a distraction every time they decided to cry, randomly shriek, or scream-sing the lyrics to a Wiggles song.

This was going to be a long ride. I tried to ignore my rumbling tummy and focus my mind on tomorrow's Eid celebrations. Our Eid plans included waking up early with the family and heading to the local community hall for Eid prayers, followed by a big breakfast of falafel, hummus, fresh bread—

"Toilet!" Adam wailed. "Number one and number three!"

"Number *three*?" Dad cried out, alarmed. "What's that?"

Adam didn't have time to explain. "Toilet!"

Mum groaned. "Why didn't you go when we stopped?!"

Adam just looked at her blankly, as if she'd asked a silly question. After all, why would he go at the nice clean service station where we had stopped half an hour ago when he could wait until we were on a lonely stretch of road with only cows, sheep, and landscape on either side of us to declare he wanted to do a *number three*?

Dad pulled the car over to the side, grabbed the packet of wet wipes, and took Adam out. Hannah looked out the window and started listing all her favorite foods. My stomach moaned.

"Chocolate donuts, ice cream, lollies—"

"Mum, this is torture. Can I walk?"

"Butterflies taste with their feet," Noor announced to nobody in particular. I ignored him, and he kept on reading.

"Can we just dump the kids at some playland tomorrow?" I asked Mum. "That way we can spend Eid with Teta and Gedo without the high blood pressure."

"High blood pressure." Mum chuckled. "You're thirteen, not thirty."

"These kids are *killing* me."

"You don't mean that, Deyana. Think positive thoughts. We're nearly there."

"There's seven hours to go. Can you at least give me extra credit on my phone when we arrive? As a reward for putting up with these brats?"

"Insha'Allah."

"I guarantee it's *God's will* that I have more phone credit, Mum."

"Insha'Allah."

"You're not fooling me. We all know what a Mum Insha'Allah means."

"Deyana, be patient, and it will increase your reward—HANNAH, GET YOUR HEAD INSIDE

THE CAR AND PUT YOUR SEAT BELT BACK ON! DON'T YOU DARE DO THAT AGAIN—WE ARE ON A HIGHWAY! MY GOD, CAN WE HAVE ONE, JUST ONE, MOMENT OF PEACE?!"

Mum stopped, out of breath. She looked at me sheepishly.

"Insha'Allah," I said with a grin.

Iftaar time at last. We sat in a highway restaurant, our table overloaded with greasy, unhealthy fast food. Heaven.

I glanced at my parents. They looked exhausted.

"Bet this road trip was a breeze when it was just me, hey, Mum and Dad?"

"I wouldn't have it any other way," my mum said as she calmly removed the tissue Adam had shoved up his nose.

"Yeah, right," I scoffed.

Hannah squirted ketchup onto Dad's lap.

Mum automatically handed him Adam's tissue.

"It's true," Dad said stoically as he mopped his lap.

I rolled my eyes at the ceiling.

Dad looked at his watch. The Azaan app was counting down the seconds till the call to prayer. Four, three, two, one, go!

Noor put down his book. We both reached for a fry, and Dad gave us "the look."

"Double D first, kids."

I raced through the dua, scarfed down a date Mum had brought along, and then, just as I was about to shove a bunch of hot, salty fries into my mouth, Hannah loudly declared, "Adam farted."

"Did not."

"Did too."

"Did not."

"Yes, you did."

"No, I didn't. I did *two* farts!" They both collapsed into a fit of giggles.

Mum, Dad, and Noor couldn't help themselves and burst out laughing. I just scowled, ate my food, and tried to think of being alone on a long stretch of beach, surrounded only by the sound of crashing waves.

Four hours down. Four hours to go.

Mum was driving now because she'd clearly had enough of her passenger parenting duties—catching things Adam and Hannah randomly threw, finding a clean tissue/water bottle/snack/tiny Lego piece Hannah needed *now*, playing YouTube DJ to four children with four very different musical tastes.

Dad was only fifteen minutes in. So he was still cheerfully and naively optimistic and competitively trying to prove to Mum that managing us kids was *easy*. He started with a "Let's play quiet brain games to try and get Adam and Hannah to doze off naturally like sweet angels" strategy.

"Right, who can name as many interesting things about chewing gum as they can think of?"

Adam got in first! "It's sticky and—"

Noor cut him off. "Too easy! It's the oldest candy in the world. Thousands of years ago, people chewed stuff that came out of plants. In prehistoric times, they chewed on stuff from trees. To clean their teeth and have nice breath. They probably needed it after all those wild animals they ate! Bubble gum was invented in 1906. Juicy Fruit and spearmint were really popular flavors and still are. Spearmint, peppermint, and cinnamon are the most popular in the world. Oh, and the first bubble gum color was pink!"

Wow. I was impressed. Secretly, of course. I wasn't going to give Noor the satisfaction. So I just rolled my eyes at him.

"Excellent, Noor," Dad said. "What about Adam or Hannah?"

Adam and Hannah were both drawing now. But they were great multitaskers.

"I want pink bubble gum," Adam wailed as he colored.

"Me too!" Hannah added as she drew.

"WE WANT PINK BUBBLE GUM! PINK BUB-BLE GUM! WE WANT PINK BUBBLE GUM!"

I looked at Mum. She was grinning at Dad triumphantly.

Dad wasn't giving up. He put on a big fake smile. "Okay, Insha'Allah! But for now, how about we list all the things we love about Eid? Adam, you go first."

Hannah obviously wasn't allowing that. "No, I will. Presents! Money! Presents! Wrapping paper! Presents!"

"What about family?" Dad said.

"Presents!" Adam said.

And then Hannah and Adam spent the next ten minutes singing, "We love presents and pink bubble gum!" at the top of their voices.

Dad slumped down into his seat, folded his arms, and closed his eyes. "Don't these kids ever get tired?" he muttered.

Mum gave him the *I told you so* look.

"Insha'Allah!" I added.

They both groaned at me.

"Are we there yet?"

"No."

"Are we there yet?"
"No."

"Are we there yet?"
"No."

"Are we there yet?"
"Yes!"

I rubbed my eyes and looked out the window. There was my grandparents' blue house with the yellow shutters and white pebble path to the front door. Mum pulled into the driveway, put the car in park, and almost threw herself out the door. Dad was even faster and had pretty much jumped out as we drove in. He was already unloading the trunk. I turned to wake Noor, who was sleeping deeply, still clutching his book. I took off my seat belt and jumped into the middle seat. Hannah and Adam were snoring, little mouths open, eyes shut tight. I looked from right to left, left to right. No doubt they were plotting against us in their sleep. I wanted so badly to feel excited about Eid. The big family gatherings, presents, and food. Breakfast after a month of fasting! But as guilty as it made me feel, I couldn't relax, knowing all our energy would be sucked up by my annoying siblings.

My grandparents were at the car now, grinning wildly. They opened the door, and I climbed over Hannah and threw myself into their outstretched arms.

"Eid Mubarak!" they cried.

I hugged them tightly.

Noor woke up and jumped out of the car and into their arms. Dad came and gently took Adam out of his car seat. Adam snuggled into his chest but stayed asleep.

"Can you get Hannah?" Dad asked.

"Fine," I muttered.

I leaned into the car to reach for her when I noticed a piece of paper that had dropped to the floor: Hannah's sprawling writing and Adam's stick figure pictures.

> *deer Deyana and Noor*
> > *we love you mutch becoz you are owr big*
> *sista and big brotha*
> > *Happi Eed*
> > *Adam and Hannah*

They'd drawn a picture of all four of us inside a big heart. I felt all my frustration fade away, and a surge of love for them overtook me.

I picked up the card and carefully placed it on the

seat. I unbuckled Hannah and gently kissed her cheek. She clasped her hands around my neck. "Deyana, I want pink bubble gum," she whispered, half asleep. "I want presents and ice cream and Eid."

"Me too, baby girl," I whispered back.

"RAMADAN MUBARAK!"

"OUCH!"

I woke up the next morning to Hannah and Adam using my body as a trampoline. Noor, already showered and dressed, was sitting on his perfectly made bed beside us, reading the new book our grandparents had given him last night (*1,001 MORE Random Facts*—I dreaded the return trip).

"You can eat! You can eat!" Hannah chanted.

"Here," Adam declared, and he shoved a piece of bread into my mouth.

I sat up, spluttering, and spat the bread out.

"Adam! I could have choked!"

Adam looked at the remaining piece of bread in his hand and threw it behind his back. It hit Noor in the face, sending Adam and Hannah into fits of hysterics.

Noor simply picked up the bread and popped it into his mouth.

"Food. In the day. Yum," he said, and continued reading.

I forgot about my near-choking experience and was suddenly giddy with excitement.

"Eid!" I cried, grabbing Hannah's and Adam's hands and leading them in a dance around the bedroom.

"Come on, Noor!" I cried, grabbing his hand too and dragging him away from his book.

He grinned, threw the book on the bed, and joined us.

"Pancakes!" I sang. "Ice cream! Lollies—"

"Cold water when you're thirsty!" Noor cried.

"Beach trips with Teta and Gedo!"

"Presents!" Hannah shouted.

"More presents!" Adam yelled.

"EID!"

We jumped up and down and then collapsed onto the floor, giggling and panting as we caught our breath.

Hannah turned her face toward mine. "Deyana?" she said.

"Yes, baby girl?"

"Are we going to have a fun Eid?"

I sat up and smiled at my siblings.

"Insha'Allah!" I said.

And this time, I meant it.

ACKNOWLEDGMENTS

A Feast—*in thanks*

We must lay out a spread of the special Eid foods mentioned in this anthology to acknowledge the wonderful people who helped us bring this project to life.

One heaping bowl of jollof rice for Erica Finkel, our editor, who loved the idea of a celebratory anthology the very moment she heard of it.

Two steaming plates of chicken biryani for our agents Taylor Martindale and John Cusick, our cheerleaders from the get-go.

Three orders of fried plantains for Emily Daluga, Hana Nakamura, and Andrew Smith and everyone at Abrams Kids, who made it possible for our idea to become a book held in our hands.

A dinner of lontong and fish fry, followed by a dessert of brownies, donuts and ka'ak for each of our contributors, our dream team: Jamilah Thompkins-Bigelow, Asmaa Hussein, Candice Mongomery, Rukhsana Khan, Hena Khan, G. Willow Wilson, Sara Alfageeh, N. H. Senzai, Ashley Franklin, Hanna Alkaf, Huda Al-Marashi, Ayesha Mattu, and Randa Abdel-Fattah.

Frosted cupcakes for Zareen Jaffery for leading the way, for carving space for Muslim stories in children's publishing.

Aisha: Three servings of gulab jaman for my children, Waleed, Musa, and Zayn, the lights of my life.

Sajidah: Mugs of hot chocolate for my children, Hamza, Jochua, and Bilqis, for all the days of Eid joy we've shared, evolving as the years went by from the excitement of waking up to presents on Eid mornings to our Eid nights now ending in a long bout of Super Smash Bros.

Aisha: A dish of lamb stew for my husband, Kashif, my support and strength in all things.

Sajidah: A bean pie for my husband, Jez, because I tried my first most delicious one with you the year we got married, and life has been good since, alhamdulillah.

Several tall glasses of mango juice for librarians, all of

you who make way for stories like the ones in this anthology, who made us believe there would be people to embrace them.

Bags of cotton candy for the teachers who champion books that serve as mirrors and windows, books that help kids both find themselves and meet new friends. Thank you for growing lifelong readers.

Packs of pink bubble gum for our readers ready to appreciate the world in all its big, beautifully diverse glory as presented in our stories. You keep us writing.

CONTRIBUTOR BIOGRAPHIES

Randa Abdel-Fattah is a prominent Australian Muslim Palestinian academic and anti-racism advocate and the multi-award-winning author of eleven books. Her young adult and children's books have been published in more than sixteen countries. She is currently adapting her debut novel, *Does My Head Look Big in This?*, as a feature film.

Sara Alfageeh is a Jordanian American illustrator and creative director. She is passionate about history, teaching, girls with swords, and the spaces where art and identity intersect. Her clients sprawl from comic designers to filmmakers, including credits with the BBC, Harvard, and Star Wars, among others. Find Sara's work at sara-alfa.com.

S. K. Ali is the author of two young adult novels, *Love from A to Z* and the 2018 Morris Award finalist, *Saints and Misfits*, which won critical acclaim for its portrayal of an unapologetic Muslim American teen's life. Her picture book, *The Proudest Blue*, coauthored with Olympic medalist Ibtihaj Muhammad, is a story about resilience. She has a degree in creative writing and has written about Muslim life for various media outlets, including the *Toronto Star* and *NBC News*.

Hanna Alkaf is the author of *The Weight of Our Sky* and a graduate of Northwestern University's journalism school. She spent more than ten years writing everything from B2B marketing e-mails to investigative feature articles, from nonprofit press releases to corporate brochures, until she finally realized that what she really wanted to do with her life was, to paraphrase Neil Gaiman, make things up and write them down. Hanna lives near Kuala Lumpur with her husband, their two children, and a mountain of books.

Ashley Franklin feels more comfortable sitting with a pen than standing at a podium. Fittingly for her personality, she's a children's author and online college instructor who dabbles in writing from time to time. *Not Quite Snow White* was her picture book debut with Harper-Collins. She resides with her family in Arkansas.

Asmaa Hussein is the author of numerous children's books like *Bismillah Soup, Mr. Gamal's Gratitude Glasses*, and *Who Will Help Me Make Iftar?* Asmaa currently runs a small Canadian publishing company (www.ruqayas

bookshelf.com) focusing on children's books that feature Muslim characters. She lives in Toronto with her daughter, Ruqaya.

Hena Khan is the author of the highly acclaimed middle grade novel *Amina's Voice*; the Zayd Saleem Chasing the Dream series: *Power Forward, On Point,* and *Bounce Back*; and her newest release, *More to the Story.* She also wrote several groundbreaking picture books including *Golden Domes and Silver Lanterns*; *It's Ramadan, Curious George*; and *Under My Hijab.* Hena grew up celebrating Eid with her Pakistani American family in Maryland, where she still lives today. You can learn more about her at www .henakhan.com and connect with her @henakhanbooks.

Rukhsana Khan is an award-winning author and storyteller who has published thirteen books. *Big Red Lollipop*, her most famous book, was chosen by the New York Public Library as one of the hundred greatest books from the last hundred years.

Huda Al-Marashi is the author of the memoir *First Comes Marriage: My Not-So-Typical American Love Story.* Her other writing has appeared in the *Washington Post*, the *LA Times, Al Jazeera, SELF,* the *New York Post*, and elsewhere. She lives in California with her husband and their three children. Visit her at www.hudaalmarashi.com.

Ayesha Mattu is the editor of two groundbreaking anthologies, *Love, InshAllah: The Secret Love Lives of American Muslim Women* and *Salaam, Love: American Muslim Men on Love, Sex, and Intimacy*, featured globally in media from the *New York Times* to the *Jakarta Post*. Her essays have appeared in the *Washington Post*, the Establishment, the *Good Girls Marry Doctors* anthology, and elsewhere. She writes, paints, and drinks copious cups of chai in her beloved city, San Francisco.

Candice Montgomery is the author of the young adult novels *Home and Away* and *By Any Means Necessary*, both of which feature intersectional Black teens. When not writing, she can be found teaching kids to dance or doing a little of the same herself.

Aisha Saeed enjoys writing for all ages. She is the author of the young adult novel *Written in the Stars* (Penguin, 2015), the *New York Times* bestselling middle grade novel, *Amal Unbound* (Penguin, 2018), and the picture book *Bilal Cooks Daal* (Simon & Schuster, 2019). Aisha is also a founding member of the nonprofit We Need Diverse Books. She lives in Atlanta, Georgia, with her husband and sons.

N. H. Senzai is the author of award-winning books that focus on the immigrant and refugee experience, including *Shooting Kabul* and *Escape from Aleppo*. She lives in the San Francisco Bay Area with her husband, son, and a cat who owns them. Visit her online at www .nhsenzai.com.

Jamilah Thompkins-Bigelow is a lifelong educator with experience working both as an English teacher and a director of writing programs for youth. As a writer, she is best known for her picture books, including the critically praised, ALA Notable Book *Mommy's Khimar*. She was raised in Philadelphia by an immigrant mother of the Mandinka Muslim culture and a Black American father who converted to Islam. She enjoys celebrating those cultures and all things Philly in the stories she writes.

G. Willow Wilson is the author of the *New York Times* bestselling comic book series Ms. Marvel, winner of the 2015 Hugo Award for Best Graphic Story. Her first novel, *Alif the Unseen*, was a *New York Times* Notable Book of 2012, long-listed for the Women's Prize for Fiction (formerly the Orange Prize), and winner of the World Fantasy Award for Best Novel. At San Diego Comic-Con, it was announced that Willow would take over writing duties on the ongoing Wonder Woman comic book series in November 2018.